From the Deep Forest

Don Shearer

Published by Don Shearer

Copyright © 2017 Don Shearer

This is a work of fiction. Names, characters, places and incidents are either the product of the author's imagination or are used fictitiously, and any resemblance to actual persons, living or dead, business establishments, events or locales is entirely coincidental.

No oversized, mysterious primates or middle school students were harmed during the composition of this work.

FROM THE DEEP FOREST

Illustration and cover design, including Chapter 3 Sasquatch portrait, copyright © 2017 by Brian Cundle

ISBN: 978-1543039801

PRINTED IN THE UNITED STATES OF AMERICA

For young readers and anyone who remembers what it was like to traipse around the woods with an open mind.

For Barbara, whose perpetual enthusiasm for exploring
the wonders of furry beasts never ceases to inspire.

There often exists, just beyond our reach, the presence of a curious mystery that visits our imaginations both day and night. And then, on a rare occasion, we get a brief glimpse of its reality, and we are forever changed.

CONTENTS

1 – MOTION

Very early on a quiet sunny morning deep in the woods of the Pacific Northwest, a solitary deer munches on some tasty ferns. The sun is coming up, changing the aspect of the forest, so once this snack is done it will be time to move on to find the next safe spot. The deer freezes momentarily as it listens for a possible sound in the woods. Ruling out a threat, it resumes feeding. The deer goes around a large tree to munch on the plants from a different angle, and there notices a large tree that didn't seem to be there before. The deer again stands still, looking up slightly to assess the situation. In a flash the deer realizes this large object is no tree. In fact, two huge hairy arms and hands extend out of it. The deer's day is about to go quickly downhill.

"You goof!" said 13-year-old Crystal McKenzie to her little brother, Freddie.

On this warm spring day, Freddie had been practicing his pitching against the brick garage wall with a tennis ball, and he didn't make any particular effort to miss Crystal as she rode out of the garage on her bike. Crystal was a cheerful girl much of the time—but certainly not right now. The ball hit her on the right hip with a pop and rolled back toward Freddie.

"Well, if you didn't interrupt my game, you wouldn't get plunked," retorted Freddie. He said this from the bright sun about 40 feet from where the driveway met the house. Freddie was a thin, sandy-haired boy of eleven who loved books, baseball and adventure.

"I'm going to plunk *you* next time, but maybe with a cinder block," Crystal added with irritation as she rode past Freddie and down the driveway to visit a neighborhood friend.

"Yeah, we'll see," he said, closing the dialogue on the topic of clobbering one's kin.

The McKenzie house stood on a cul de sac at the end of a street that wound through a deeply wooded area of Cherryville in northern Oregon. The McKenzies had a long, straight driveway that came in off the court, leading to a modest-size suburban house set in front of trees that towered over the house. Their back yard wasn't terribly large in overall space, but what it lacked in surface area it more than made up for in surroundings: tall, lush, shapely trees came right up to the edge of their property, forming a wall of deep green—a virtual back yard gateway into the quiet woods.

At better moments, Crystal and Freddie were able to spend time together without much nastiness or associated tennis ball targeting. When temporarily removed from the ever-invading influence of peer forces, Crystal, a fairly tall, brown-haired girl just entering the rocky teen landscape, was able to tolerate Freddie's little-brother annoyances rather well. They would sometimes trade creative ideas for pastimes in this quiet little corner of Cherryville. They were likely nearing the end of their days of sibling play, but not quite yet.

Despite the occasional dustup, the two kids enjoyed taking walks together into the forest to explore and have new adventures. This part of the country was lush with green growth and plenty of water to nourish it. There were the big trees—firs, spruce, hemlocks, cedar, oaks, birches and more. In the understory of the forest, there was plenty of undergrowth of shrubs and berry-laden plants to provide food and cover for the many animals living here. The kids would spot, observe and catalogue animals whenever possible. They'd see turtles and rabbits and chipmunks and deer and a rare bobcat or coyote. They would notice old trails that hunters probably used long ago. Every once in a while they'd find a colorful shotgun shell or an old bottle next to the trail. It often rained quite heavily, but on dry days the sunlight shone gracefully down through the high green canopy, illuminating a fairly teeming wonderland of life.

One time they happened upon an inviting, comfortable curve in a stream and decided to get down in the mud and construct a big two-foot-high earthen levee to dam up the water. When the water backed up nearly to the top, they simultaneously jumped on and kicked at the dam, opening gaping gaps and letting loose a little wall of water that cascaded down the newly bare streambed. Dabbling in some hydro-engineering in the woods could be fun.

Another good example of forest engineering was an idea that Freddie first had. At this point the brother and sister were spending a fair amount of time in the woods together, and Freddie said it might be good if they had a fort or hideout structure in the woods that they could call their own. They agreed it would be nice to have a little woodsy getaway where they could hang out, either individually or together (when they could manage to put up with each other), away from the supervisory gaze of parents. Sometimes they would talk about what kind of structure they would build, and they started visiting their dad's large scrap woodpile at the side of the house to scavenge for building materials.

"I think we should build a fort with four walls, a roof and maybe a front door," suggested Freddie one day.

"Do you think Dad has enough old wood out here to build something?" Crystal asked.

"Well, he might," said Freddie. "He's got a lot of old plywood and other boards. And whatever we need beyond Dad's supply we might be able to 'borrow' from that half-finished construction site down the street," said Freddie.

About a year before, someone had cleared a lot and started the foundation for a single family house, but for some reason the construction stopped and a few stacks of concrete blocks and weather-beaten boards sat unused. The abandoned project would support others' plans now.

Crystal came up with a schematic drawing for the sibling structure. It was pretty basic, consisting of two plywood 4x8s serving as the parallel walls, with another 4x8 serving as a flat roof atop the walls. A few 2x4s nailed in at key spots would serve as wall support, with the walls in turn supporting the 4x8 roof.

They agreed on the admittedly crude design, and as school was ending for the year they got started on their building project.

With their dad's permission, the kids selected four slightly waterlogged plywood 4x8s and stacked them on top of a wagon. Together they awkwardly pulled the wagon a few hundred feet into the woods to the fort site. They had also collected a few old, mismatched 2x4s that they carried in a second wagon load. A can of nails and a few tools including a little hand saw completed their inventory of building supplies.

After a few clumsy early blunders whereby Freddie let go of and dropped a 4x8 before Crystal could get nails into it, they wrestled with the wood enough to eventually put the frame together and get the walls and roof to stand. A good strong wind or maybe a big angry bird could probably knock the whole structure to the ground in a heap, but the kids didn't worry about that too much.

With the two walls in place, Freddie suggested that they wall off a third side of the fort as well—the one that faced back toward the house. They wouldn't need much privacy out here in the woods, but the extra wall seemed like a good idea. A plywood 4x8 cut in half would do the trick, and it would also provide some extra roof support.

They grabbed a few stray cinder blocks from the construction site and pulled them in the wagon to the fort. They placed them strategically around the bottom of the wood walls for additional support.

After suitably finishing the structure, the kids managed to slip away every few days after school to visit the fort for a few hours. Soon they began to bring a few items out to furnish the place—some old kiddie chairs to sit on, a big plastic bucket turned upside down to serve as a table, some rope on which to swing from a nearby tree, etc. Freddie or Crystal would bring other items out once in a while, such as a ceramic garden gnome or a sports team bobble head doll to put in or on top of the fort. The place wasn't real comfortable or attractive, but at least it was *their* place.

One of Crystal's favorite pastimes was playing guitar and singing, so she began to carry her acoustic guitar out to the fort sometimes so she could practice in the natural comfort of the deep woods. Crystal could play a few folk song standards, plus the refrains of some current pop songs, but she really liked writing her own little ditties. The woods were a good place to try out the new material, and Crystal appreciated the open space and lack of an audience for her compositional experiments. Along with the six-string guitar accompaniment, Crystal's clear, gentle voice nicely serenaded the woods.

Freddie, however, didn't hesitate to play the woodlands critic. After one of Crystal's renditions of Proud Mary, he said, "You know, you're going to injure some poor mammal or mollusk with that stuff."

"Hmmph!" Crystal replied sharply. Her brother's clearly cruel critique would not prevent her from singing her songs in this sylvan setting.

The area of the fort was close enough to home to be comfortable, but just far enough away to represent its own little world where the customs and routines of busy human life didn't mean much. The silence was soothing, caressed only by the breeze that rustled through the leaves of the tall trees all around.

Every so often when they were out doing something at the fort, they would hear the distant snap of a branch or what sounded like some far-off leaf crunching. One time Freddie thought he heard a knock on a tree from some distance away. Often one or the other of the kids would take a look out into the forest, but there was no one there.

Once when they came to the fort a few days after a rain, Crystal spotted what she thought was a very large footprint in the worn dirt area right in front of the fort. Both of the kids stared and puzzled at the shape, but it was not very distinct and didn't make much of an impression on them.

When walking out to the fort a few weeks after that, Freddie noticed an odd assembly of broken tree branches standing up about sixty feet to the right of their well-worn trail. With some imagination, it looked a little like the branches had been arrayed as a fairly large, orderly, standing X shape. But it was entirely possible that the rain or wind had caused the branches to fall into that position. It was cool looking but it seemed entirely natural.

An event that somewhat changed their view of the woods occurred very late on a Saturday night in June. The family had a movie night with snacks and drinks in their comfy great room that was populated by plush, low couches and two recliners, with framed images depicting rural life and nature scenes adorning the walls. After the movie ended and the empty popcorn bowls were herded into the sink, everyone headed slowly off to bed. It was a very comfortable early summer night, and the parents and Freddie had their windows open to the mild evening.

An hour or two after everyone had gone to sleep, the three family members with open windows were more or less simultaneously awakened to hear a long, mournful howl from some distance away. As Freddie awoke, he thought the sound resembled a single blast of an old fire engine horn or air raid-type siren, with the pitch rising slowly to a peak then going back down into silence. Though it wasn't close by, the sound was certainly loud enough to wake those who had open windows. The deep silence after the howl faded out was intense.

"Uh," asked Mr. McKenzie groggily, "did you hear that?"

After a few moments, his wife said, "Yes. What on earth was it?"

Mr. McKenzie said, "I don't know. It's been a long time since I heard something like that. I thought at first it was coyotes, but they're usually in a pack and there are a bunch of different sounds. This one was by itself."

Each of the listeners—Mr. and Mrs. McKenzie and Freddie—lay still amidst their own thoughts, pondering the source of the sound. Regardless of its origin, the unique and mysterious cry from far out in the night gave each individual a chill. Sleep didn't arrive again very quickly or comfortably for anyone.

The next morning over a waffle breakfast, they all let Crystal in on the experience. She listened intently and considered their accounts.

"Now, you be careful out in those woods," Mrs. McKenzie said sternly to both the kids as they were putting breakfast dishes in the sink.

The summer moved on and in a week or so the kids were back out at the fort. The indoor pastimes of video games and occasional visits with friends kept Freddie and Crystal entertained for only so long. The freedom of the woods eventually beckoned.

One late summer day, they were at the fort reenacting a medieval battle, with Freddie as an attacking marauder shooting rubber-tipped arrows at Crystal, who was protecting the noble castle (i.e., the ungainly wooden fort) armed with a plastic hand-held battle shield and a less-than-imposing, highly non-medieval tennis racket.

"I hereby use my great archery skills to destroy and subdue your kingdom," said Freddie in a stilted, highfalutin' voice. Upon issuing this warning, he pulled back his bow and fired a little arrow which shot wildly up into the trees. Its errant flight threatened little more than whatever insects were perched on the closest tree branches at that moment.

"You, sir ridiculous knight, couldn't hit the side of a barn" said Crystal dismissively.

Undaunted by the harsh criticism, Freddie continued to fire arrows toward Crystal. Most of Freddie's volleys were highly misguided, spinning harmlessly away from the fort into the leaves. If a rare shot got within three feet or so of Crystal, she would easily bat the arrow down with the shield or the tennis racket.

But after Freddie had fired all his arrows and retrieved them to refill his quiver several times, one of his shots surprisingly hit home as Crystal moved around the side of the fort. She had started to lose some interest in the incoming projectiles, but this time one caught her flush on the left ear. She was not pleased.

"Ow, you stupid idiot!" she said. "Those things hurt."

She rubbed her ear for a few seconds, then put her head down and retreated into the fort to hide her embarrassment at being picked off by one of Freddie's shots. The arrow stung a bit more than she wanted to admit.

"What did you expect?" he asked. "I told you I would totally destroy your kingdom." He bent down and followed Crystal into the fort.

She replied, "You should have waited until I was ready. Just get out of here."

"Hey, I'm the winner of this war, so you need to cough up your official surrender and give me the keys to the whole kingdom." He was clearly riffing on the theme of battle victory. Crystal didn't really want to hear it.

"Screw you, stupid goof!" Crystal said very loudly, pushing Freddie backward toward the fort entrance. He fell onto his butt in a sitting position.

Just as Freddie fell, both kids were startled and frozen in place by an incredibly deep growl from well outside the fort. The huge sound was immediately shocking and disorienting. The low sound hit them flush in their chests.

The growl felt like a barely controlled tidal wave to the kids. Or maybe a whole set of heavy knives hitting their chests at once. Or maybe five or six of their fort's cinder blocks pounding them right in the midsection. It was that powerful. Every nerve in their bodies was instantly overwhelmed.

For a split second, Freddie thought of the sound that he'd heard big male lions make at the zoo. Crystal said later that she thought it sounded like a cross between a bear and one of those massive dump trucks she'd seen on TV rumbling around strip mines.

Whatever it was, the sound was clearly sending a message. Something out there was very angry. And it wasn't very far away. The kids' shock quickly turned to utter fear—quaking, primal terror.

If that wasn't bad enough, only a few seconds later there was a huge crash on the roof of the fort right next to their heads. Both kids hit the deck after this very close explosion of sound. A big rock or a whole tree or something must have hit the fort, Crystal thought. The entire structure shook a little bit, after which something seemed to drop to the ground next to the fort.

Lying parallel in the dirt, Crystal and Freddie looked at each other as if for the last time, completely mystified about what had just happened, and of course wondering who was making all that noise and clearly trying to end their lives. Neither child made a sound as they clung to the ground in profound fear of imminent attack. They listened to each other's breath rush in and out.

Over the course of several minutes they tried to recover from the shocking events, and as their senses slowly revived they realized that the near complete silence of the woods had reasserted itself. If they were going to be killed, at least it wouldn't be right away.

"What is that smell?" Crystal asked quietly, not really expecting a response. A very foul stench had overtaken the fort, adding to the sensory overload with which the kids were currently dealing.

"Maybe it's a killer skunk or something," said Freddie. "Our luck doesn't seem to be too good right now."

They lay still for several more minutes. Nothing was happening. Crystal was the first one motivated to move enough to perhaps look out the front door. No, that was unthinkable. But yes, they'd have to look; they couldn't stay in the fort the rest of the day—maybe their last day on earth.

She crawled forward silently until her head was about at the opening of the fort. She slowly rose to her knees to try to look around. Freddie remained flat and unmoving on the dirt floor of the structure. He was not particularly enjoying the awful odor of the killer skunk, or whatever it was that was stinking up the place.

As Crystal tentatively scanned the area, nothing outside really looked changed. Someone was certainly there a few minutes ago, but there was no one in sight right now. All the big pines stood just where they did before, and no big leafy trees had fallen over. The afternoon sun came quietly through the leaves and pine needles at the exact same angle as it did a few minutes ago. No big boulders or strip mine dump trucks had rolled crazily into the area and struck their fort. All was silent and still. What on earth was going on?

Crystal then crawled out of the fort and stepped in front of it to get a wider look at the area. She looked back around the right side of the fort and saw nothing. She turned and looked around the left side, and to her surprise there was a medium-sized branch lying next to the structure. One end of it looked freshly shredded or twisted. This must be what had struck the fort with such a crash.

She didn't think about how this could have happened or why; she just wanted to figure out if they were safe now. She was not yet convinced.

"Uh, somebody threw a big branch at us," she reported to Freddie.

"A branch? What the heck?" he replied.

Crystal said, "It looks like it got broken off and thrown or something."

Freddie thought about that for a moment then offered a sly suggestion. "Maybe next time you can block it with your tennis racket," he said.

Largely ignoring that comment, Crystal now looked further out into the forest. She scanned from right to left, trying to see if anyone might be peering out at them from behind one of the big trees. Nothing looked unusual, except that when Crystal looked well out to the left front of the fort, one tree caught her eye.

Or maybe it was just a large stump. But wait a minute—had it been there before? Crystal's brain spun quickly as she tried to figure out if there was a stump or fat tree in that spot before. She wasn't sure. Quickly she ducked back into the fort to try to seek a second opinion.

"Freddie, I want you to come out and look at this big stump," she ordered.

"No way," he instantly replied. "I'm not coming out. I really don't feel like dying today."

"You're not going to die," she said. "At least not before I'm done with you," she added tartly. "I just want you to tell me if this thing was there before."

Freddie again asserted, "I don't want to."

"Oh come on," Crystal urged, grabbing him by the left arm and pulling him to the fort entrance. Freddie reluctantly crawled forward and stood up, looking around with eyes squinted as if the sky was about to fall on his head.

"Over there," Crystal said while pointing to where she first spotted the woodsy shape. Freddie looked in the direction that Crystal pointed. He didn't see anything unusual.

"I only see *the same dumb woods we always see*," he said with exasperation. "I have no idea what you're talking about."

Crystal looked again at the stump or tree, but it was...gone.

"I, I don't know where it is!" she exclaimed. "It was right over there."

"Like I said, I have no idea what you're talking about," said Freddie. "Can we get out of here now? This place is way too scary and stinky for me."

Crystal just stood still and stared at the spot. This was another of the many odd little situations that the kids had encountered over the last few months. But in the midst of today's mysterious uproar, the vanishing tree took on extra import.

"I really don't know what's going on," Crystal said with a confounded tone. "There was something there a minute ago and now it's gone. This is crazy."

Freddie immediately piled on. "No, what's crazy is our staying here."

Crystal continued to stand and ponder the situation. She had no answers. She had no bright ideas about what to do next. All she knew was that a little time had passed since they heard the growl and got bashed by the branch, and maybe by now it was time to get home.

The two kids stood and looked around the area for another minute or two. They heard the "ooh, ooh, ooh" of a barred owl call not too far away. The sound seemed to bring them back to earth just a little bit. Now Crystal was ready.

"Okay then. Let's go," she said nervously. And they did.

Standing closer together while walking than they normally ever would, Freddie and Crystal quickly put it in gear and, side by side, made a beeline down the trail toward their house. Their quickened gait was just below that of a run. It was, perhaps, a fast walk with plenty of urgency, just in case something might be following them.

Freddie looked back just once, but fortunately didn't see or hear anything.

2 - BUSYNESS

Little more than an hour after dawn, near a grouping of residential buildings, several young humans walk from different directions to a central location where they stand together. Most of them carry bulky pouches on their backs. Each individual is quiet as he or she approaches the meeting place, but as more small humans gather, they begin to chatter. Some make unexplainable noises. Some stand silently, tapping on small hand-held devices that fully consume their attention. One small individual taps on his device as he walks, and bangs noisily into a thin vertical structure topped by a large, flat shape with lettering. Two of the waiting individuals seem somewhat familiar. Soon a big, loud, bright yellow rolling object arrives. One by one the individuals climb up and disappear into an opening in the front of the object, then the portal closes and the object rolls away. After this, silence returns. Strange creatures, these humans.

It was a Monday morning during the first month of school. Both Crystal and Freddie attended Monroe Junior High, a slightly aging school about five miles from their house. With the weekly grind resuming, it was time for Crystal and Freddie to get their heads in the game of learning, but neither of them was much in the mood for concentration. The sights and sounds (not to mention smells) of their weekend adventure in the woods still gripped them pretty tightly.

"Freddie, please hurry and finish with breakfast so you can print out your assignment," Mrs. McKenzie said to Freddie.

Freddie was groggily slumped over his cereal bowl. His mother's orders jolted him a bit. He slurped up the last of his Frosted Tweetie-O's, finished a small glass of orange juice, and walked over to the family office area (a corner of the dining room) to plug his flash drive into the computer and print out his weekend homework essay for U.S. History. It was a few paragraphs he had to write about the Hoover Dam, that great public works edifice of the desert West.

Freddie considered the words comprising his situation, and an opportunity dawned on him. "I didn't like this dam assignment," he said expectantly, in advance of the predictable parental disapproval.

"Language, Freddie," his dad scolded.

"Well that's what it *is*," Freddie retorted.

"Okay, just get it into your folder and finish packing up. It's getting late," Mrs. McKenzie said.

Mr. McKenzie, a nearly middle-aged man sitting at the kitchen table in his business casual polo shirt and khakis, went back to reading the sports page on his e-reader.

Freddie sluggishly put his jacket on and scooped up his backpack, lunch and trumpet case. (He had band class in 5th period.) Crystal had already finished eating and getting her stuff together, and was ready to head out the front door to the bus stop.

"It's cold this morning, Crystal," yelled out her mom, catching up to her. "You should wear a jacket."

"No, I'm good," asserted Crystal. "Besides, my jacket's dirty. It's in the laundry."

"Well...wear this other one," said Mrs. McKenzie, hurriedly reaching into the front closet and handing Crystal an old Albuquerque Isotopes baseball jacket that Mr. McKenzie had picked up on a business trip to the Southwest a few years back. The red jacket featured Orbit, the team mascot, who was some sort of crazy orange dancing bear gone goggly-eyed via exposure to excess radiation, or something like that.

"I'm not wearing that thing—it's *hideous*," said Crystal as she wriggled away from her mother.

"Come on, it's getting cold out, and you'll be LATE!" Mom said forcefully.

Crystal fired back, "No, I don't want to!"

"Go!" said Mom, pretty much pushing Crystal out the front door with the baseball jacket flung over one shoulder.

Freddie scuttled out afterward, following well behind Crystal down the sidewalk to the driveway.

"Have...a good day," Mrs. McKenzie said rather weakly from the porch as the kids headed down the driveway to the front court. She sipped her slightly cold coffee as she went back in the house.

"You know, these mornings aren't getting any easier," she said to Mr. McKenzie at the table, perhaps hoping for a bit of spousal support.

"Do you know," he began, "that the Mariners are 14 games out of first place right now? Completely out of it."

Mrs. McKenzie looked at him with some exasperation. "I think maybe *you're* the one who's completely out of it, dear," she said with mock affection.

He continued unmoved. "I'm glad the Seahawks games have started; at least they're not in the basement yet." For Mr. McKenzie, the annual kickoff of football season would have to once again replace the summer's discontent over a lengthy, lackluster baseball campaign.

Mrs. McKenzie sighed and headed over to the sink.

Crystal got to the bus stop first; Freddie still lagged well behind. A couple of girls were chatting quietly, and they giggled once in a while. Crystal went over to join them.

Freddie stood by himself and observed the approach of Trevor Weldon, a slight, glasses-wearing boy with whom Freddie shared some level of geeky, friendly comfort. As usual, Trevor was typing on his phone as he walked. On this day, however, when he was almost to the bus stop, he walked smack into the yellow No Outlet sign. He fell back on his butt and his glasses went askew on his face. He rubbed his face and straightened out his glasses. The sign wobbled back and forth for a moment as if struck by a windstorm. Trevor then stood back up. A bunch of the kids, including Freddie, got a good laugh at Trevor's painful encounter with suburban signage.

Luis Martin, a wiry, slightly smart-alecky kid with close-cropped blond hair, started hurling funny noises toward the group of girls. "We-be-dweeby we-be-dweeby we-be-dweeby," he said in the most grating, sing-song tone he could conjure at this early hour. The girls tried to ignore him as usual.

Angela Kravetz, the bossiest of the other girls in the group, took a good look at Crystal and couldn't resist ribbing her. "Ooh, nice jacket, Bozo girl," she said with high sarcasm. The other girls giggled some more.

"In fact," she went on, "that's one for the world to see." With that she pulled out a pink smartphone and snapped a picture of Crystal in her Orbit-wear before Crystal even knew what was happening.

"I'll just post this to Facebook now," Angela said smugly as she uploaded the photo to her page. "I'll caption it 'Crystal and her Bozo Coat.'"

"Oh God," said Crystal, panicked, dreading life right now. "*Really*?"

The gaggle of girls giggled again.

Soon Mikey Menton, the largest, burliest and loudest of the bus stop boys, sauntered over stealthily and quickly snatched Freddie's trumpet case from him without saying a word.

"Hey," Freddie yelled at Mikey. "Give it back."

Mikey, sporting close-cropped hair and wearing a pro football team jacket, turned and lumbered off, out of reach of Freddie's reflex grasp.

"But we all want a concert!" he shouted to the whole group, and to no one in particular. He opened the latches on the trumpet case and pulled out the horn.

"Mikey, give it!" exclaimed Freddie again. But it was too late. Mikey had slipped the mouthpiece onto the trumpet and put the instrument up to his face. He aimed it into the sky and blew into it with gusto.

The resulting blast of noise was absurd and completely out of place in an otherwise civilized location at 7:45 a.m. Freddie, duly horrified at the latest instance of Menton morning shenanigans, thought the sound resembled a crazed, drunken elephant. Trevor Weldon, looking up from his phone, thought the noise sounded like a loud warbling fart from the sky.

Mikey had now attracted ample attention, so he kept things going. After the initial sonic atrocity he started dancing around like an alien lounge musician from the first Star Wars movie, blasting dangerously uncontrolled rude sounds into the otherwise quiet morning air.

Mr. Garcia, wearing a sweat suit and sneakers, was out for his morning jog with his springer spaniel Josie on a leash, running closely next to him. Man and dog both briefly regarded Menton's outburst, then continued on their way without any particular reaction. Middle school kids sometimes seemed like creatures from another planet.

Determined to end the ridiculous din, Freddie grabbed the trumpet back from Mikey, cleaned it off and put it back in his case. Mikey was highly skilled at playing the crowd buffoon, but he also had a nasty side that came out sometimes. Freddie was pleased to have retrieved his trumpet without further incident. Undoubtedly the neighbors were also pleased.

Not a great start to the week, Freddie thought.

At Monroe, the kids worked their way through the first school day of the week. Crystal thought that most of her 8th grade classes were pretty easy, and she largely floated through the day with the casual confidence of the typical upperclassman—she was ready to move on to bigger and better things in high school next year.

Moving through the hallways over the course of that Monday, Crystal thought she observed some knowing snickers from a few other girls in her grade. She chalked it up to the fact that Angela had elevated her to a status of social media infamy via the unfortunate Orbit jacket photo. Like most kids at that age, Crystal had to develop a pretty thick skin in order to survive the daily cruelties of middle school peers.

Freddie also did his best to get back in the game, and his interest in the day's proceedings didn't really gel until he got to Earth Science class in 6th period. Though the topic of Mr. Milanovich's class today was global climate change, Freddie was still somewhat in the thrall of the past weekend's events. As Mr. Milanovich wrapped up projecting some photos of scientists measuring ice shelf depths in the arctic, Freddie kicked off a highly unrelated line of inquiry. He put his hand up.

"Question, Mr. McKenzie?" asked Mr. Milanovich, in a smooth, assured voice. He was one of the cooler teachers at Monroe, speaking to the kids not so much as children but as young geek colleagues.

Freddie started with, "Are there any unexplained large predators living in the area?"

Mr. Milanovich, tall with dark curly hair, regarded Freddie over his glasses for a moment, letting the out-of-context nature of Freddie's question settle a bit over the classroom.

"I assume you're not referring to the arctic, Mr. McKenzie," responded the teacher dryly.

Freddie continued, "I mean right around here, in the Cascade Range."

Mr. Milanovich was well aware of the living spectrum of animal life in the region, both real and mythologized. "Well, there are polar bears at the top of the chain," said Mr. Milanovich, "but they're so far pretty well explained. Of...course the infamous Sasquatch has a winter cottage down here," continued Mr. Milanovich with more color in his voice, "but he prefers the as-yet frozen expanses up north in the summer, where he goes by the nickname Yeti, Freddie."

Most of the class broke up with laughter over the cleverness of their teacher's response.

Freddie remained undaunted in his quest for answers.

"I guess I mean right around here, within a few miles of the school," he continued.

Mr. Milanovich again regarded Freddie with a lowered gaze over his glasses, and said, "Mr. McKenzie, I believe the only large unexplained creature in our midst is Mr. Menton over here."

The class really got a good laugh at this one. Freddie realized that his own interests were not within the topical limits of the class this day, so he dropped further questions.

As the class was breaking up and the last students were exiting the room, Freddie spontaneously stopped by Mr. Milanovich's desk up front.

"Ah, the ever intrepid Mr. McKenzie," the teacher announced summarily.

Freddie's voice was much quieter now. "Uh, Mr. Milanovich, I'd really like to know if there have been reports of anything weird lately," he began. "My sister and I had...an experience...the other day."

Barely missing a beat, Mr. Milanovich said, "Yes, the veggie surprise was somewhat shocking at the cafeteria on Friday." With that he could quickly see Freddie's disappointment over not being able to address an apparently pressing issue.

"Okay, what's your concern, young meister?" he asked with a bit more seriousness.

"Well, Crystal and I were out in the woods behind our house this weekend, and we heard the growl of something really big," he explained. "Plus I think it threw a branch at us."

Mr. Milanovich considered this account for a few seconds. Then, as most teachers do who need to wrap up and move on to their next class, he offered some closing explanation.

"There are a lot of things it could have been," Mr. Milanovich said. "Occasionally one of the big cats or a bear will come down from the upper elevations looking for food. They're not usually noisy, but you never know. That doesn't really explain the throwing part of your...experience; that one may have to remain a mystery for now. Keep me apprised of what you find out there," he said.

"I will, thanks," said Freddie in a rather dejected tone as kids in the next class were streaming in past the desk.

Although he liked to have some fun with his students, ultimately Mr. Milanovich didn't want to put the kibosh on Freddie's curiosity. He said, "Look, I appreciate your interest, Freddie, and since I think I know what you're really talking about, I don't mind if you ask me about it. I have an interest in—shall we say—unique creatures, and I've certainly heard lots of things about the Big Guy over the years. So keep me in the loop."

This made Freddie feel at least somewhat better. When you're dealing with something that's potentially off-the-charts weird, it helps to have whatever kind of ally you can find.

Freddie walked out and headed for U.S. History.

One school day evening after dinner later that week, Crystal was walking down the long driveway to retrieve the family's mail from the box. As do most young people, she was texting with a friend as she walked. Crystal and friend Sara were discussing the relative merits of the flexed biceps of a lead singer in one of their favorite pop music groups, the Outrageous Noodle Bombs. Crystal reached the mailbox, extracted a few letters and a small parcel package, and closed the mailbox door.

Looking up to start heading back, something caught her eye far over to the right between the Fosters' and Schneiders' houses. Like the McKenzie house, these other two-story dwellings on the court were spread fairly far apart from each other, and they all shared the dark green backdrop of big trees behind them, though the McKenzie's trees were taller and more densely packed. Mr. Schneider was an avid gardener, and in his back yard were the remnants of this past summer's small corn crop, green bean vines and big tomato plants supported by cylindrical wire frames.

It was getting dark out, but Crystal could see someone standing behind the dried-up corn stalks. This didn't seem unusual at first, until Crystal's brain began kicking in and processing the presence of the unfamiliar individual, maybe 600 feet away.

Crystal started thinking of how corn stalks could easily be seven or eight feet tall. So the head of the person she was seeing would have to be well higher than that; in addition to the face, some wide shoulders were visible. But the odd thing was that the face and shoulders were all dark. Despite the late hour in the evening, she thought she should have been able to see the person's face. So, strangely, she couldn't make out any features to determine who it could be.

Whoever it was, this individual was clearly looking directly at her, standing rock still behind the dry stalks. Halloween was just a few weeks away, Crystal quickly reasoned, so maybe this was someone in a gorilla or King Kong costume. But it just didn't add up. Why would someone be in Mr. Schneider's back yard in a costume at this hour? Plus, the person was *way* taller than any of her classmates or the few older teens in the area. This person had to be huge.

With all of this occurring to Crystal within just a few seconds, she experienced an uncomfortable stab of fear and decided to get back inside. She briefly glanced down to arrange the stack of mail and the phone in her hands, then took one last look at the large person behind the Schneiders' house. There was no one there.

Crystal was inside the house less than 15 seconds later.

A few nights after that, the McKenzie's beagle, Marty, was making a bit more of a baying racket than usual out behind the house after dark. Mr. McKenzie was reading and he noticed the canine hoot-fest.

From his comfy chair in the family room, he said to Freddie over by the TV, "Hey man, go let Marty in, please."

After a few seconds' delay, Freddie hit "pause" on his battle-goths video game. He stood up from in front of the TV, stretched, and headed for the sliding glass back door. He went outside onto the back porch where Marty's barking was clearly making quite a racket.

"Marty, knock it off," he said to the small tricolor dog, who was at the end of his tie-up tether, hooting aimlessly at the woods, it seemed.

Freddie walked over to him and was about to unclip him so he could guide him by the collar back into the house. Freddie looked out in the direction that Marty was barking and saw nothing but the usual huge black wall of nighttime trees. There were also two small red or orange lights, fairly close together, about ten feet high by Freddie's estimate. Freddie unclipped Marty and turned around. A bit hunched over, he started walking the dog back to the house.

Reaching the back door, Freddie realized that he had no idea at all why there would be reddish lights in the trees. They weren't all that bright; they were just fixed in place, facing the house.

Freddie slid open the back door and gently shoved Marty inside. Then, hesitating, he slid the door closed and remained outside. He looked back to where the lights were. He could still see them, unchanged. He walked out just a bit on the porch, continuing to look at the lights, when they both went black. This stopped Freddie in his tracks. Then the lights immediately came back on.

This was fairly weird, thought Freddie. But what finished the job for him was when the lights started moving slowly, in tandem, to Freddie's right. Just as they did that, there was a fairly loud crack of a branch break. Now the red lights turned off and stayed off.

Freddie's heart started racing, and he turned and jogged nervously toward the sliding door. He did not look back.

3 – REVELATION

The two small humans who built the woodland structure seemed a little less loud and strange than some of the other individuals in the immediate area. The young male in this pair was observed trying to quiet a small, overly noisy canine, and, fortunately, was able to corral the creature back inside the family's dwelling. The young female in the pair, though often staring down into her hand-held device like all the other humans, would sometimes walk by herself to the end of her family's front pathway, and sometimes to another dwelling close by. More so than many of the other humans, these two seemed inclined to spend time outside of their boxy places of residence and their rolling vehicles. Perhaps contact with them would result in a minimum of risk.

Despite the kids' recent experiences of getting slightly spooked, life continued as usual for them at school and home. Dad was still obsessing over the unseemly end of the Mariners' baseball season, as

Mom continued in her usual efforts to keep the household wheels on the cart.

At school, the first quarter of the year was proceeding predictably. Mikey Menton was sent to the office from U.S. History class one day for hitting Jeff Karsdens over the head repeatedly with a large classroom globe. Another time he stole Jimmy Werner's sack lunch and put it under the non-petite Leah Zeilinski just as she sat down at her desk, instantly obliterating the lunch and creating a gloppy mess beneath the deeply mortified Leah. Mikey and his minions howled with glee at the squishy outcome.

After some time without visits to the woods, and no more scares from any source (other than perhaps Mikey Menton), Crystal and Freddie eventually resumed their forays into the forest. Fortunately the hideout was only a few hundred feet back in the woods behind their house, and the short trips there soon became routine again.

"I don't think Jeff enjoyed getting bashed in the head by the whole world," Freddie explained to Crystal when they were hanging out at the fort one slightly cloudy day. "I'm starting to think that Mikey should probably just go straight to the office first thing in the morning and spend all day every day there."

"Yeah, I'm pretty glad he doesn't know we've got this place," Crystal replied.

Freddie thought about that statement for a moment, and added, "I don't think he'd find a lot of value in being out here. There's no audience for his crazy crap other than a few squirrels and deer."

Crystal and Freddie then heard two very distinct knocks on a tree. They stopped and looked at each other.

"What the heck was that?" said Freddie.

"I don't know," said Crystal, "but there's definitely someone out here."

She crawled to the front of the fort with Freddie close behind, and at the entrance they both stood up and scanned the area to see if they could spot the source of the noise. Being inside the fort, they couldn't tell which direction the sound came from. They looked in every direction. There was no one in sight.

But then, over in the direction from which Crystal thought she saw something during their previous fort adventure, Freddie noticed that one of the big trees was…moving. From this angle he could only see the lower portion of it, as all the upper branches of this tree were blocked by other low trees that were closer to the fort. Freddie strained to get a better look.

He then saw that the tree was slowly coming straight toward them from a few hundred feet away, and it was walking. On legs. Freddie then noticed two huge arms hanging straight down. And as the tree moved clear of other trees that had been blocking it, Freddie could see a large dark head atop the "trunk" of the tree, which was, in fact, a huge barrel chest and body, all covered in very dark hair.

With his heart suddenly pounding like mad and his arm and finger pointing straight outward, Freddie slowly and clearly said everything that was needed: "There he is."

Crystal immediately saw what Freddie was pointing at, and she froze with shock as the figure continued slowly toward them.

It was essentially a man, but covered in dark hair instead of clothes, and much, much larger than a typical man. The face was a bit lighter colored than the rest of the creature, and the top of the head sloped backward and somewhat came to a point. There was no visible neck; the creature's shoulders seemed to angle up into the back of the head. The face looked rather serious in expression, although at this distance at least, not particularly aggressive. The nose appeared broad and rather flat, and the piercing eyes were topped with heavy brows. The arms were huge and very muscular. The shoulders were incredibly wide, seemingly three or more feet across. The hands, hanging down to the level of the creature's knees, looked like the size of large baseball mitts. The legs were wide and powerful. Long, stringy-looking dark brown or black hair streamed down from around the face and chin, and everything but the center of the face was covered by the dark hair.

The reality of what they were seeing hit each child like a falling ton of bricks. The local legends, the mysterious night sounds, the fleeting sightings, the curious footprint evidence—all clearly pointed to the real deal now. Along with this recognition, of course, came a well justified jolt of complete terror.

"We're gonna die now, aren't we?" asked Freddie very quietly, without moving an inch.

Crystal struggled to find something to say. "Uh, maybe. Yes. I don't know. Oh, my God," she said with a trembling voice.

She moved closer to Freddie and grabbed onto him as she never had before. He instantly grabbed back and they clung to each other as if waiting for a tsunami to strike and flatten them. They stood literally quivering in fear of what they were seeing. And it was getting closer. Although their flight response was just about to overcome them, how could they possibly get away from something so clearly huge and powerful?

Now only about 50 feet away from them, the creature was carrying a short, thick stick of wood. It must have been using this branch to make the tree knock sounds. It walked very slowly, calmly and deliberately toward them, and the kids weren't sure if the creature was trying to not terrify them too much, or if it was just stalking them slowly like a big cat does as it approaches its prey—right before attacking with an explosion of lethal violence.

But instead of attacking, the creature stopped, stooped, and with extreme gentleness, laid the broken-off tree branch down at its huge feet. It then stood up to its full height again, arms at its sides. It stood totally still now, looking at the kids rather blankly as if waiting to see if they were going to scream and run away or not.

Virtually every instinct within the kids told them to run as fast and as far away as they could, shrieking like wild things until someone—anyone—came to rescue them from this incredible danger. But something, perhaps the calmness of the creature, perhaps some underlying fascination with what they were seeing, or perhaps simple shock, kept them from turning and bolting for their lives.

It was almost like the creature was putting the ball in their court now, but neither Freddie nor Crystal had any idea at all what to do with it.

As the quiet stare-down continued, Crystal tried to coax her brain away from overwhelming thoughts of certain death, to a slightly more logical assessment of the situation. She looked more deeply at this creature than at anything she had seen in her life. She soon figured that not only was this creature extremely tall, but it was utterly and completely massive. Its monstrously thick limbs and body were so far outside of human scale that they boggled the mind. Quickly gauging the creature's size against nearby trees and the occasional boulder in the background, Crystal estimated that it must be somewhere up to nine feet tall and weigh anywhere from 500 to 800 pounds. Or maybe it was 1,000 pounds. Who could be sure when something that tall was also thick and solid? Calculations at this moment were pretty meaningless.

As the creature moved slowly closer—again, not in a threatening way—both kids noticed the novel feeling of having to crane their necks back in order to look someone in the eye. It was a bit like the disorienting first moments of sitting down in the front row of a theater when the screen images seem a bit too close and tall. This figure was definitely too close and tall.

The creature was definitely the biggest biped that they—or probably anyone else on the planet— had ever seen. Its long dark face simply looked down at them without any display of emotion.

Despite the still silence, Crystal and Freddie remained rather unconvinced that they would survive this encounter. Their bodies continued to quake, with all senses on high alert in front of the mysterious, silent giant. Soon their senses delivered additional input: a powerful stench resembling the smell of rotten eggs, old seafood trash and a skunk all rolled together. This huge creature stunk beyond measure. The whiff of a scent they had smelled previously was now a veritable punch in the nose given the close distance between the giant and the kids at this moment. If the shock and terror were not so great, someone would have commented harshly on this foul odor.

Without any further communication, the creature simply turned and began walking away slowly to its left. It took very measured, unhurried steps as it moved away from the kids. They stood transfixed. The creature turned and looked back at them just once as it walked. Soon it seemed to speed up as it moved deeper into the shadows of the woods. The kids realized that it was making surprisingly little noise, particularly since it was such a massive creature, and it almost seemed to glide away through the forest. When Crystal and Freddie last saw it, it was moving very quickly, its shape starting to blend into the trees as it passed. And just like that it was completely gone.

The kids remained riveted to the ground, clearly still in shock at their experience.

"Can you believe it?" said Crystal.

Freddie said, "I, uh, I think I wet myself."

"Oh...I *definitely* wet myself," concurred Crystal.

"That has got to be the stinkiest thing ever," added Freddie.

"It could have killed us like houseflies. I have no idea why it didn't," said Crystal with quiet gravity.

"Maybe it was late for five dinners or something," reasoned Freddie.

"It's...like it was almost trying to communicate or at least just watch us. It looked like it was trying real hard to move slowly," Crystal said.

"Yeah, and did you see how fast it disappeared when it decided to go? I don't know how something that big can move quietly, but it did," said Freddie.

"I just can't believe that we saw this creature and it pretty much presented itself to us," said Crystal after a few moments, still mystified by the creature's behavior. "What do you think we should do?" she asked.

"I can't wait to tell Trevor...and Mr. Milanovich," said Freddie. "They'll flip out. And probably Mom and Dad too," he said.

"Oh no," Crystal said right away. "We need to think this through first. It may not be good to tell everyone about it."

"I wanna tell everyone I know, plus go on TV tonight and get famous," countered Freddie, without much subtlety.

Crystal came down hard on him. "I said *no*! To begin with, no one's going to believe us, and if they do, they'll probably send out a hunting party with a couple thousand guns.

I...just don't know," she trailed off.

Freddie didn't know either. Everything was kind of a blur right now.

Crystal said, "Well, maybe it's time to get home."

"Okay. Let's go," said Freddie.

The brother and sister started walking down the trail toward their house. Pretty much simultaneously, each child's walk became a jog, and soon a flat-out run, as they headed for home.

Mr. and Mrs. McKenzie could clearly tell that something was amiss for Freddie and Crystal at dinner that night. By the time he was partway through his spaghetti, Freddie couldn't contain himself any longer.

"We saw something out in the woods today," he began, casually.

Mom and Dad stopped their munching for a moment to regard the kids.

"Yes, it was a big green ogre with fangs," said Crystal almost immediately. She scowled at Freddie for having tipped the lid back.

"An ogre, huh?" asked Mr. McKenzie. "I think I knew one of those once, but she divorced your grandpa."

"Very funny," responded Mrs. McKenzie, knowing that the reference was to Mrs. McKenzie's mother. "So what did you see out there?" she asked.

Freddie continued amidst Crystal's disapproving scowls. "It was your average huge monster. You wouldn't believe it," he said.

"I'm pretty sure it was an alien ogre," resumed Crystal, working at spinning the account into an absurd corner. "I think it...traveled here from a green planet looking for spaghetti or something."

"Well it sure came to the right place. This stuff is really good," said Mr. McKenzie. "Maybe we can make him an ogre bag so he can take some pasta home with him."

Mr. McKenzie rarely missed a beat when it came to the absurd. For once, Crystal was pleased with where things ended up.

For the rest of dinner, Freddie frowned at Crystal and worked on his spaghetti in a downcast fashion. He knew that fully sharing the events of today would probably have to wait a bit.

Over the next few days, Crystal and Freddie didn't say too much to each other about their encounter, but having shared something so remarkable seemed to close them off in their own exclusive world to some extent. They were slightly more distant from friends and family. It was unlikely that anyone could really grasp what had happened to them.

Before long their natural curiosity began to work on them. In their quiet conversations they started to reference the fort, and maybe going back out there sometime. The thought was scary and enticing at the same time. They talked about it on and off for a couple of days.

Then in the garage one day after school, they were again discussing the fort and their "friend," and at one point Crystal said, "You know, let's just go."

And they did.

In the coming days they had a couple of entirely uneventful but quite brief visits to the fort, basically testing the waters to see if everything was going to be okay. It seemed that way, at least.

One day Freddie had an idea. He walked far out in front of the fort and looked around. He saw what he was after and went over to it. It was the branch that the creature had broken off. Freddie walked back toward the fort with the branch, and then went over to the closest big tree. He gave the branch two big swings, sounding out two fairly loud tree knocks. The sound echoed out over the forest, startling Crystal with its volume.

"What are you *doing*?!" she asked.

"I dunno," replied Freddie. "Talking, I guess."

The kids stood still, listening, the branch down at Freddie's side. They didn't do anything for a few minutes, just listening as intensely as they could. They heard only the wind caressing the leaves of the tall trees, and an occasional bird call.

After a few more minutes they heard a rustling far off in the woods, and in a few seconds they saw the familiar huge shape arrive and then stop several hundred feet away. It stood and looked at the kids as it had previously. Again there was no aggression or other intention that they could perceive. The creature's mere presence at a distance of several hundred feet spoke adequate volumes.

Freddie didn't know what to do at this point, so he just quietly dropped the branch as the creature had done during their last encounter.

The creature was watching very closely and seemed to move slightly in reaction to Freddie's gesture. It walked a few feet to its right and picked up a branch from the forest floor. It effortlessly broke off the smaller end of the branch and walked over to a nearby large tree. Looking straight at the kids, the creature took two swift swings resulting in loud tree knocks. On the second knock, the branch shattered into pieces, with wood shrapnel shooting all around. Freddie's immediate thought was that it would be great if this creature could put on a Seattle Mariners jersey and give the team's offense a jolt with some power hitting.

Kids and creature stood looking at each other for a few more minutes. Then the creature turned and gracefully vanished through the woods just as it did the first time.

"Well, *that* was pretty cool," said Crystal, still staring off where the creature had left her field of vision.

"I don't think he has a lot to say," asserted Freddie, "but who cares?"

Certainly neither Crystal nor Freddie cared about the creature's apparent lack of expressiveness. They had found their own way to get through to him.

4 - COMMUNION

The two human children had begun to adopt one of the standard methods of forest communication. They seemed somewhat uneasy in their motions, but that was not uncommon for humans who have unexpectedly encountered an apex predator that fully dwarfs them. Typically, most humans run away in fear or reach for their hand-held shooting devices for protection. Little do they realize how futile these measures would be if the large forest dweller decided to truly engage them. Regardless, the small male and female were proving agreeable, and some continued interaction with them seemed reasonable. However, these humans were not entirely self-sufficient in the wild; occasionally they placed themselves in situations requiring intervention.

Now that their comfort with being in the woods was starting to resume, Crystal and Freddie began visiting their fort a bit more often. What had been a sense of unsettling fear gradually transformed into more of a curious anticipation of what they would next experience in the forest. Each of the kids started looking forward to opportunities to head out together and spend a little free time at the fort after school.

Soon Crystal wanted to try Freddie's technique of tree knocking. Freddie figured that the available arsenal of sound-producing branches in the vicinity of the fort was pretty limited. So, being a dabbler in the baseball arts, Freddie brought one of his small wooden bats out with them one day. Crystal said she wanted to do the knocks this day, so Freddie handed her the bat.

"Try not to hurt yourself," he said dryly.

"If anyone's going to get hurt, it will be you," she replied forcefully. "You know, you're starting to look an awful lot like a tree...so hold still!" she said as she feigned a swing at Freddie.

"Just you try it," he warned.

With that, Crystal went up to the closest tree and took several robust swings. The bat made a much louder and tonally resonant "crack" than the dried-up tree branch from the forest floor that Freddie had used previously.

After the knocks had been issued, the kids followed their usual pattern of standing still and listening. A few minutes later the expected result began to occur. They heard the distant rustling of leaves, and before long, their very large forest counterpart came into view and stopped—as usual—several hundred feet from them.

"You know, I never get tired of this," said Freddie.

Every few days the kids would venture out to the fort to try their newfound communication technique. The tree knocks were successful pretty much every time, although the length of time it took for the creature to appear would vary. Sometimes the creature appeared within 30 seconds or a minute; other times it would be five or six minutes before the kids heard anything. Regardless, the tree knocks were proving a pretty reliable way to make contact. The creature's apparent respect for space between itself and the kids made them increasingly comfortable.

One time Freddie took his usual two bat swings, and after waiting for a while, nothing happened. The kids waited outside next to the fort and looked around for nearly ten minutes, with no response.

Mildly disappointed, they eventually went inside the fort to attend to other topics.

About fifteen minutes later they heard two very assertive knocks from out in the woods. Quickly looking up at each other with eager smiles, they scrambled out of the fort with anticipation to check things out. Sure enough, a few hundred feet away stood their oversized companion, casually tossing aside a big branch as the kids viewed him. The creature reminded Freddie a little bit of a very large ballplayer who had just homered, flipping the little bat away with satisfaction.

"Should we have doubted him?" Crystal asked reflexively.

Late one afternoon, Freddie was by himself in the back yard playing a solo game of pretend baseball, substituting a tennis ball and his imagination for a real baseball game. He would toss the ball a few feet high in front of him, and belt it fungo-style out into the yard toward the big trees. A sharp liner would equate to a single. A longer, hard-hit shot that bounced to the first row of trees— probably a double. Only when a ball made it into the upper tree branches and stayed there, without bouncing back into the yard, would it be a home run.

In his imaginary contests, Freddie always had the Mariners play some other pro baseball team. Sometimes it was the Anaheim Angels. Sometimes it was the dreaded New York Yankees from the distant East Coast. Using a handful of tennis balls, Freddie would essentially keep score, differentiating the clean hits from the lazy fly balls or short pop flies, counting up the runs inning by inning until the outcome was decided. Usually, through some miracle of lightly engineered competition, the hometown Mariners would come out on top.

The light was fading on this day, and Freddie's mom came a few steps out onto the porch to call him in for dinner. "I'll be there in a minute," Freddie said with some impatience, the parental summons never quite coming at a good point in the game. He sped up the pace of his game as the ninth inning played out. His Mariners were still down a couple of runs to the Yankees, and Freddie would have to bang out some quick extra base hits in order to subdue the pinstriped archenemy.

A left-handed batter, Freddie made good contact and whacked a double to right, the ball landing about twenty feet from the trees and rolling to them.

"It's a double. Runners on second and third; Mariners still down by two," said Freddie, the imaginary hometown broadcaster.

"Freddie, dinner!" yelled Freddie's Mom, with her head poked out the door. Then, a good bit louder, she added, "*Now!*"

Freddie replied, "Okay, okay." The pressure was on. Freddie tossed up a faded yellow ball and took a mighty cut, but caught nothing but air. He almost fell over with the force of the swing. "Two strikes on Robinson Cano," he said with urgency. It was now or never. Another "pitch" from the Yankee reliever came in. Freddie whacked this one well, the ball arcing high and deep and disappearing into the top branches at the edge of the yard. It did not come back.

"It's a three-run shot for Cano!" called out Freddie, dancing around a little at the dramatic triumph. Adding some slightly snarky color commentary, he said, "The Yankees will have to hurry to catch their flight back to New York. Today's hero Robinson Cano will remain here in Seattle."

Meanwhile, Freddie had to hurry to get himself inside for dinner. He ran back to the house. He would have to retrieve the game-winning home run ball later.

The next day was Sunday, a bright, blue-sky fall day, and Crystal was in the little historic downtown district of Cherryville with her good friend Rebecca. Crystal's dad had dropped them off for a few hours of wandering and browsing through the old shops on the town's main street. There was also the prospect of some good coffee and ice cream shops where yummy treats could make the day sweeter.

Crystal and Rebecca, a cute, lanky redhead, were in one of the brownstone-fronted old shops looking at inexpensive jewelry pieces to add to their evolving wardrobes. The smell of exotic incense wafted through the store, which was one of those fun gift/book/accessory shops with an airy, angelic feel. As Rebecca inspired giggles in both girls when trying on a funny long-eared hat, Crystal spotted Ms. Turner, a somewhat free-spirited middle-aged woman who was Crystal's music teacher a few years ago.

Crystal thought about this situation for a moment, and said to Rebecca, "Hey, why don't you go back and check out those cool earrings we saw in the front window, and I'll catch up with you in a minute."

Rebecca looked at Crystal without quite grasping the instruction, but soon she put the pink long-eared wool doggie cap back on its hook and said, "Okay, I guess I'll be up there." She walked slowly toward the front of the store, browsing aimlessly as she went.

Ms. Turner still was right on the other side of the display rack, so Crystal simply said, "Hi, Ms. Turner."

The slightly stocky woman with short, strawberry blonde hair and wearing a colorful tie-dye shirt, regarded Crystal as most people do who are seeing someone out of context and can't immediately place them. She looked over her glasses at the young girl but didn't say anything.

Seeing Ms. Turner's lack of recognition, Crystal explained, "It's Crystal, Crystal McKenzie."

"Oh, Crystal, well *hello girl*!" said the teacher with increasing zest. "Are you playing much guitar these days?" she asked.

"A little bit," replied Crystal. "School keeps me pretty busy. We have a lot more homework than we did at Timber Grove." This was the elementary school where Ms. Turner taught music.

"Yes, yes, you're in the big time at Monroe now. Well don't forget to pull that guitar out and keep playing and writing. That song about turtles you wrote with Jane Murray was *way* cool," she reminded Crystal.

While this was true, and probably worthy of further discussion, Crystal didn't want to get too bogged down since Rebecca was essentially waiting for her up front.

Crystal asked the teacher fairly excitedly, "Hey, do you remember that news story about the Cherryville Monster that you brought in one day?" This was a distinct memory that Crystal recalled, as the newspaper story of a Sasquatch sighting pretty close to home had attracted Ms. Turner's interest considerably, and in turn caught the interest of all her music students that day.

Crystal continued her line of questioning. "Do you think the legend is real?" she asked Ms. Turner.

"Um, yes, sure, I do remember that," said Ms. Turner, almost certainly caught off guard by the lack of context for Crystal's questions. "And I do believe

Bigfoot is real" added Ms. Turner. She was a bit of a sandals-wearing nature lover who enjoyed all kinds of music and was quite open to things like the paranormal and mystical creatures.

Several years earlier, something nicknamed the Cherryville Monster had apparently been spotted several times within a few days—once near a campground, once in a cornfield at the edge of a farm, and once by a small group of hikers who encountered a large creature upon returning to town on some backcountry trails. The local papers picked up the story, and it was a weird news diversion for several days around the region. After the series of encounters near Cherryville, the creature wasn't seen again.

"Well, Freddie and I uh...we...um, might have seen that thing, or something like it" said Crystal.

Ms. Turner regarded Crystal with some alarm. "Really?!" she asked in an urgent but suddenly hushed tone. "What makes you say it might be the Cherryville Monster?"

"It was maybe eight or nine feet tall, covered in dark hair, very smelly and just overall huge, really," Crystal summed up.

"Wow. Are you sure? Where did you see it?" asked Ms. Turner.

"Actually it was only a few hundred yards back in the woods behind our house," Crystal explained.

Ms. Turner just stood still for a few seconds to ponder the magnitude of Crystal's report.

"Oh my *gosh*. Did you see it well or did it just disappear as they usually do?" Ms. Turner asked.

Crystal giggled just a little. "Freddie and I have seen it a bunch of times in the past few weeks, and we communicate with it using tree knocks," she added without flair.

"A bunch of times?! Tree knocks?! Good heavens, Crystal, this...this is incredible. Are you sure about this? If it's true, you've really got something on your hands there," said Ms. Turner.

"Oh it's true all right," asserted Crystal, confidently. She could see Ms. Turner trying to absorb and process the information.

"Well, if it's not too scary, maybe you should try to get some photos or video...some documented evidence," Ms. Turner suggested.

"I never really thought about that," replied Crystal. "I guess I could do that, but I wouldn't want to spook him," she added. "We're pretty used to him now and I don't know how he would react if we brought gadgets out into the woods."

"You're…used to him…" Ms. Turner said, and her voice trailed off.

"Even though we've been communicating for a while," Crystal continued, "it's been from pretty far away, and I'm not sure what to do next."

Ms. Turner thought about that point for a moment, and offered a suggestion. "So, this guy is a big mammal, right? Hmmmm. A big and strong and stinky Sasquatch?" she added with glee. "Well, every overgrown mammal loves a big snack now and then; why don't you put some treats out for him and see how that goes?" she said.

As Ms. Turner was issuing her suggestion about appealing to the dietary interests of the creature, Crystal noticed that Rebecca had quietly returned to the back of the store. She was standing a few feet away, looking at Crystal with raised eyebrows and a near laugh on her lips.

"Um, I guess Rebecca and I should get going," Crystal said to Ms. Turner.

The teacher said, "Oh hi, Rebecca" and reached into her purse for something. "Here's my card, Crystal. If you get some good evidence, please email or text me. I'd love to see it," she said quietly. She finished with, "Take care now, honey."

"I will. See you around," Crystal said.

She gently grabbed Rebecca by the arm and led her out of the store.

Once outside on the sidewalk, Rebecca felt compelled to join the fray. "So you have a Sasquatch that you need to feed. Is this a new thing or is he a long-lost cousin or something?" she asked.

"Mmmm," Crystal growled a bit at this line of inquiry. "It's just this big creature that Freddie and I have been seeing out back," she explained.

"Oh, just a big creature," Rebecca intoned sarcastically. "I was worried maybe it was one of those dumb boys from gym class, but if it's just a big hungry creature, well okay then."

"Geez," Crystal replied with some exasperation. "It's a long story."

Crystal steered them both into a left turn off the sidewalk and went into Grandma Green's Ice Cream Grotto, where Crystal hoped to explain things somewhat to Rebecca while enjoying a decadent smoothie or over-sugared coffee drink.

Not long after, Crystal and Freddie were back out in the woods for a fort visit. But this time, in line with her plan, Crystal brought some things with her.

"You see that stump over there toward the stream?" Crystal asked Freddie. "I'm going to leave some stuff on it for the creature. Maybe he'll take it."

"Yeah, maybe," began Freddie. It didn't take him long to formulate a further comeback. "You know, I think you should probably leave your cellphone out there so the creature can text with Rebecca all day like you do," he continued. "In fact, Rebecca probably won't even know the difference of who's texting her."

"Very funny," said Crystal. Carrying a plastic bag, she walked away from the fort toward a scraggly stump to the right about 150 feet away. It was about four feet high. The much longer top portion of the old tree had broken off and now lay down across the leaves, extending outward 60 or 70 feet, which would have been the height of the tree when standing. Now the tree was rotting and serving as a comfortable loggy ecosystem for countless microorganisms. Crystal and Freddie walked toward it.

At the stump, Crystal reached into her bag and brought out some items, setting them one by one atop the stump's jagged wood top. One was a nerdy little one-eyed yellow plastic doll resembling a vertical pill capsule and wearing an oversized monocle. It was a character from the Despicable Me series of movies a number of years back.

"Oh yes," began Freddie, unable to resist the opportunity to rag on Crystal's choice of offerings. "The creature will really value that one...a great example of humanity, you've got there."

"Shut up," Crystal said sharply. She continued to bring out objects. The next one was an old Dora the Explorer doll that had likely been unearthed from the bottom of the toy box in the garage. The Dora doll had a head the shape of a football, large eyes, and brown hair with overly-straight bangs. Crystal set Dora atop the stump about a foot away from the first figure.

At this, Freddie said forcefully, "Oh my *God*. Do you want to give the poor thing a complex?"

"Just be quiet, I said," instructed Crystal. "I think he'll like this stuff."

Crystal then scooped out a small stack of chocolate chip cookies that had probably been on the pantry shelves for a while. She set them out in an array around the dolls.

"Now *that's* more like it," said Freddie.

Crystal stepped back and regarded her stumpy altar, considering it a simple yet suitable offering to the king of creatures of the forest.

"He'll probably like the cookies," summarized Freddie, "but the Despicable Dora will probably make him want to migrate to Canada or something."

"We'll see about that," said Crystal.

Though Freddie wasn't always with her, Crystal went out to the "gift stump" virtually every day, avidly hoping for a sign that the creature had shown interest in her offerings. At her first visit back, on the day after she had set out the items, there was no evidence of anyone having disturbed them other than a few ants crawling on the cookies.

The second day was different.

Upon coming up to the stump, Crystal could immediately see that the cookies had been consumed by an animal. The two doll figures remained in place. She also noticed some very large footprints in the dirt around the stump. Large toe impressions were visible in some of the prints. The creature had been here. Crystal looked all around to see if she was being observed, but saw nothing. She was pleased that she may well have contributed to the cause of Sasquatch snacking. Of course, almost any animal in the woods could have eaten the cookies, but the footprints suggested otherwise.

The next time out, Freddie accompanied Crystal to the forest. As they approached the stump, they could see that both of the doll figures were gone. Crystal was delighted.

"He took them both!" she exclaimed. "That's pretty neat."

"Yeah, I guess I'm glad he took them," began Freddie. "Those things were hideous, and maybe he can stomp them into the ground with those big feet or something."

"Uhhhh," replied Crystal with a loud discharge of air, clearly annoyed at her brother's continuing disrespect for once-beloved though clearly misshapen cartoon figures.

Since Crystal apparently had been successful with her gift stump effort, Freddie wanted to change things up during the next visit. He brought his bat this time to resume some tree knock discussion with the creature. On this sunny day, he was puttering with some items at the fort as Crystal walked ahead toward the stump. She got about halfway there and stopped abruptly, staring right at the stump.

"Uh, Freddie," she started, "I think you need to see this."

Grabbing his bat and jogging toward Crystal, Freddie looked out toward the stump and could see a small object on it. He soon caught up to Crystal, who was standing quite still. He continued running past her and got about 20 feet from the stump when he came to an exaggerated, slow-motion stop.

"Oh my God," he exclaimed as he took in the stump and the small object atop it. He walked the last few feet up to the woodsy altar and his mouth dropped open.

Right in the middle of the stump sat a faded yellow tennis ball.

At this moment Freddie realized, and Crystal soon concurred upon Freddie's explanation, that they were dealing with something far more than a primitive beast of the woods.

At lunch one day soon thereafter, Freddie saw Mr. Milanovich sitting by himself in the cafeteria, apparently working a shift as a kitchen policeman, supervising the lunchtime student mobs. Freddie thought this might be a good opportunity to broach a key subject. After he finished his lunch, he walked over to Mr. Milanovich, who was sitting on the edge of the stage at one end of the big, brightly lit multi-purpose room.

"Hey, Mr. M.," Freddie said to the teacher, who was sitting with one leg crossed over his lap, eating an apple.

"The ever-inquisitive Mr. McKenzie," the teacher said in his typical elegant tone to Freddie. "I imagine you want to hear about the latest in quantum mechanics," he added. The din of a hundred students eating lunch while chirping and throwing vegetables at each other was no small clamor to overcome.

"Well, not exactly," said Freddie. He continued undaunted. "You remember me mentioning something that my sister Crystal and I saw in the woods, right?" he asked.

"Yes, yes, I believe you saw Mr. Menton systematically threatening the lives of all forest-based mammals across the Pacific Northwest," he said colorfully.

"Um, no, you know what I'm talking about," insisted Freddie. "It's the Sasquatch."

"Ah, right, the tallest and hairiest instructor ever to grade quizzes at Monroe Middle," Mr. Milanovich said rather gleefully. Freddie laughed a bit but wasn't buying the teacher's clever banter.

"Crystal and I have seen that thing about a dozen or so times now, right near our house, and we've... traded presents with him," Freddie reported in summation.

"So, you're interfacing with some sort of...Santa Sasquatch—is that what you're telling me?" Mr. Milanovich asked, again delighting himself with his own impishness. "Isn't the Sasquatch usually too large to fit down a chimney?" he asked, fully pushing the topic off the pavement of near-logic into the ditch of zaniness.

"No, I'm *serious*," said Freddie, still smiling but emphatic. "We figured out that one of the ways he communicates is through tree knocks, and now we can actually call him and get fairly close to him in the woods."

This last set of details finally derailed Mr. Milanovich's joviality, and he regarded Freddie with a bit more seriousness.

"So you've really seen this thing and had some sort of, well, dialogue with it, huh?" he asked.

"That's right. I just wanted to tell someone who's smart that I know this creature is real, and it's sort of become...a friend of ours," Freddie added with some hesitancy. "I know it sounds crazy, but Crystal and I have found something that no one else has been able to prove, I think."

"Okay. How would you characterize its behavior?" asked Mr. M. "Is it elusive, or aggressive, or shy, or whatever?"

"Well, it's definitely a scary thing at first," Freddie explained. "The creature is about nine feet tall and three or four feet wide, so when it comes running up, you're pretty sure your life is about to end. But in our case," he continued, "it didn't seem to want to scare us all that much. It seemed more...interested," Freddie said.

"Interested," repeated Mr. Milanovich.

"That's right," said Freddie. "He could probably kill us in two seconds but he seems to enjoy...sort of talking with us... through the tree knocks. I guess he doesn't see us as any kind of threat, and we sure as heck enjoy seeing him. He stays pretty far away but he definitely seems to like the company," Freddie said.

"Fascinating," replied the teacher. "Um, Mr. Weintraub, please desist with launching the peas," he suddenly yelled very loudly over Freddie's head to another group of students he had been watching for a while.

Refocused, Mr. Milanovich continued, "I'd sure like to see this...friend of yours, Freddie. Maybe sometime I could join you and observe this massive mammal you've befriended," he said.

Freddie thought about this for a few seconds, then replied, "Maybe there's a way we can work that out."

The plan wasn't yet entirely clear to Freddie, but an idea had definitely sprouted.

That weekend, on a cool, breezy, sunny Saturday afternoon, Crystal and Freddie were walking to the house of a lady who lived near but not within their neighborhood. Mrs. Fleming, a family friend, had called the kids' mom earlier in the week to tell her she'd be out of town for a few days and asked if Crystal could come by and check on food and water for her two cats, Mr. Crusher and Puffs.

At 13, Crystal had reached the age where she was now in the informal stable of neighborhood kids who could be trusted to babysit, look after pets, and water plants. She didn't mind doing it, as there usually was a measure of payment involved. Mrs.

Fleming stopped by the McKenzie's during the week and dropped off her extra house key with Crystal's mom.

Mrs. Fleming lived one neighborhood over, so Crystal, with Freddie along on that Saturday, had to go down a connecting street between the neighborhoods. There were no houses on this deeply wooded street as it was used only for vehicle connections. Extremely tall trees came up to each side of the road, which was sunken a good bit lower than the base of the trees, so traveling this part of the road almost felt like going through a poorly lit (though quite scenic) tunnel.

As they walked along the side of the road, Crystal was telling Freddie about how she had recently resumed her guitar exploits. She had gotten together with Rebecca one evening and made all kinds of fun noise.

"We're working on a pretty cool piece," she said. "It's called 'You're a Dork and So's Your Dog,'" she offered up with some compositional pride.

"Wow," replied Freddie. "That sounds like a good one, but since it's with Rebecca, maybe you should just shorten it to, 'We're Both Dorks,'" he recommended.

"Just because you can't play anything but dumb video games on Xbox doesn't mean I should listen to you," said Crystal, defending her interests.

Coming down a slight grade, the kids then saw two brownish dogs up ahead of them on the same side of the road. Crystal put her arm out in front of Freddie and stopped him. From a distance the dogs looked like pit bulls or a similar beefy breed. Regardless, they were not on leashes, there was clearly no one with them, and they looked like potential trouble.

"This is not good," said Crystal, sounding worried.

"Oh man," said Freddie, spotting the dogs. "Where did those guys come from?"

"I don't know, but I don't like the looks of this," Crystal replied.

The dogs were somewhat jowly and bouncing off each other as they advanced toward Crystal and Freddie. Something about them didn't look right. Both dogs appeared to spot the kids at around the same time. They quickly sped up toward the kids in a manner that could only be viewed as threatening.

Freddie quickly asked, "Can we get up this hill and into these trees?" But the trees above them were extremely tall and there were no low branches to grab onto.

"I don't think so," said Crystal with rapidly increasing panic. "We need to do something!"

Freddie started looking around for some rocks or sticks he could use against the dogs, but he was running out of time fast. The dogs were only about twenty feet from them now. Crystal was working up to a scream as the dogs got right up to them, with no clear way for the kids to escape. Just as the dogs were within striking distance with teeth bared, Crystal and Freddie both heard a loud rustling and some very heavy footsteps coming up from behind them in the woods.

From the ridge about six or seven feet high right next to the road, a gigantic hairy object catapulted down and landed on the road with an immense thud. It hit the ground only about three feet in front of the kids. The entire ground shook as it landed. The kids recognized the creature instantly, of course, but were completely stunned at his appearance here. He was facing the dogs, with his gigantic arms spread out wide.

The creature then issued a sound that Crystal and Freddie had heard just once before, and it was no less shocking this time than the first, particularly given that the kids could almost touch the creature now—it was that close. The sound was an incredible, deep roar of anger that seemed to penetrate every object—living or otherwise—in the area. It only lasted about two seconds, but in an instant, all life in the area seemed to be instantly suspended amidst the rush of the powerful, monstrous blast.

The dogs stopped short as if they had hit a wall and stood wide-eyed for a moment, regarding the tall, terrifying force right in front of them. Both dogs immediately turned tail and ran off wildly in the opposite direction, squealing and whimpering as they went.

The three remaining two-legged creatures stood still where they were, watching the panicked canines retreat to where the woods ended at the next neighborhood, then running off to the left and out of sight. The big creature then turned around slowly and looked the kids over for several moments, almost seeming to assess their welfare.

They were all standing together, and with hearts racing, both Crystal and Freddie quickly realized they had never been anywhere near this close to the creature before. Looking nearly straight up at his face, the kids almost felt like they were looking at part of the forest canopy above. They were soon virtually overcome by the creature's odor. At this moment, though, it didn't seem to matter.

With a quick swing of his arms the creature then jumped back up onto the ridge with one step— an astounding feat of power and agility—and headed off quickly into the woods from the direction it came, looking back once at the kids as it began to vanish in its usual gliding fashion.

Crystal and Freddie stood in place shaking like dry leaves on a windy, late fall day (which it was, in fact). The sensory overload had the hair on the kids' arms standing up, with a deep chill having shot straight through their bones.

Everything that had happened just within the last thirty seconds was totally unexpected, and utterly shocking. If a car had been driving past at the time of the confrontation, anyone inside would have had the witness experience of a lifetime. Now silence on the road seemed deafening after the titanic ruckus that had just taken place. The kids, now quickly left by themselves, stood still and listened to the quiet forest again. The cool autumn breeze wafted gently through the leaves of the tall trees as if nothing unusual had happened.

"You know, I'm *really* starting to like that thing," Crystal said finally.

5 - PLANNING

Having barely avoided an unpleasant brush with pugnacious pooches, the young humans appeared to soon busy themselves constructing a puzzling array of odd figures and contraptions in a confined area of the woods just beyond their residence. Their attention to this exercise seemed to well exceed that of their typical forest endeavors, consuming a good bit of their time and requiring countless trips just past the tree line to carry in the unexplainable objects and position them for some untold purpose. As usual, the behavior of this species proved mostly mysterious.

During a meat loaf dinner on Sunday night, Mr. McKenzie asked the kids a seemingly simple question.

"You know, Halloween is coming up. Are you guys going to do your haunted house thing this year?" he inquired.

This otherwise harmless inquiry kicked off a series of events that could never have been foreseen by anyone within the household or beyond.

"Actually," began Crystal, "I think we're going to do a haunted *woods* this year."

This statement clearly caught Freddie off guard. He froze and looked at Crystal with some surprise, the path of his food-laden fork to his mouth having been quickly redirected by Crystal's unexpected reply.

The kids' Halloween haunted house was a veritable institution at this end of Pine View Street. For several years now at Halloween, Crystal and Freddie had spent hours rigging up a scary show for neighborhood kids in the McKenzie family's big, dark, unfinished basement. They would invite the closest of their neighbors with small children, and lead the families one by one through a highly choreographed sequence of scares consisting of ghosts, goblins and monsters, along with occasional scary noises and crude special effects designed to terrify and amuse the younger set.

Despite the kids' extensive preparation and practice, some bugs always appeared somewhere in the course of their show. During last year's haunted house, for example, when one family was led past the infamous Haunted Toilet Seat, Crystal put her gloved hand up through the seat and wiggled it menacingly as usual. Most times, this gesture reliably resulted in expressions of both fear and some shock. But last year, when Crystal pulled her hand back down, she bumped the toilet seat to the side which knocked over one of her mom's old lamps. The terrifying toilet became more of a locus of laughter.

But for this Halloween, Crystal had a different idea for the haunted display, mostly because of the increasing comfort that she and Freddie had been experiencing in the woods behind their house. Crystal theorized that by expanding the haunted house beyond their house, she and Freddie might be able to expand the scale of the thrills and chills they offered to visitors.

Once Freddie got over his surprise at the coming change in venue, he began working closely with Crystal to plan the scope and physical layout of their attractions. Initial brainstorming discussions held in the comfort of the woodsy fort soon led back inside where the kids made diagrams that they plotted with a computer graphics program, conceptually planning their series of scares.

Some of the expanded ideas they wanted to realize included having ghosts and goblins—mounted in trees and suspended from ropes or wires—that would be loosed on cue and swing down in front of the unsuspecting visitors.

Other ideas included having large spiders cross the forest floor and rush up to the visitors. This idea was great in theory but proved difficult to pull off in reality. With their mom's help, they purchased some three-foot-wide furry spiders from a nearby Halloween shop. (The store was located in a previously empty big-box retail store in town that was serving as a temporary Halloween costume and gadget warehouse.) In testing their scary spider scheme, the kids struggled to figure out how to hide behind a tree and pull the spiders along the ground via fishing wire. Tricks such as this were typically easy to pull off in the basement because the creatures and the distances they traveled were small. But in the woods, the big leggy spiders didn't slide well and mostly got crumpled when pulled upon.

Freddie then happened upon the idea of using sled-riding discs from their stock of snow sleds in the garage. They put the spider on top of the disc and tied fishing wire to a handle on one side of the disc. This allowed the spiders to slide along over the ground when pulled. Problem solved.

Other more traditional, tried-and-true scares were part of the haunted proceedings as well. A few years ago the kids' dad helped them build a small coffin-shaped box using plywood from his trusty old stash of lumber. When the families were led past the box, the lid would slowly be pushed aside and Freddie would emerge moaning in spooky Dracula-esque fashion. This year, of course, the coffin would be outside, and Freddie would have to nimbly climb inside it to be ready to pull off a well-timed scare.

Crystal and Freddie practiced the sequences repeatedly. Most often Crystal would serve as the initial host, introducing herself and the spooky attractions to the families. She would then lead them toward the first scare, which consisted of Freddie climbing eerily out of the coffin as Dork Dracula. In past years, early scares included Freddie as Frankenstein toppling out of a big old armoire, or perhaps a set of chattering teeth that Freddie would trigger from behind a couch.

This year, in the woods, the choreography would need to be refined and expanded. After fulfilling the first scare, for example, Freddie might then switch places with Crystal as host, and Crystal would then execute the next scare. This scare could be Crystal under a sheet as a ghost, popping out unexpectedly from behind a tree. All the while, scary music and sound effects would play from a nearby music player. The families would be led through the full path of the haunted circuit, at the end of which they would get one final resounding scare. Most years this was Freddie "attacking" as he growled from inside a werewolf mask, essentially chasing the family out to the exit.

As preparations continued, the kids shopped online and in stores for Halloween accessories with which to furnish their haunted woods. Mrs. McKenzie took them on several trips to the big Halloween shop nearby. The kids found lots of spooky items there. They also did some online shopping for creepy contraptions. Freddie searched through objects at an online store that sold countless Halloween items. At one point a large cardboard cutout of a Bigfoot figure caught his eye. He thought it could be a great addition to their arsenal of scares. Plus, it closely resembled a local figure with whom he was familiar... Freddie's mom helped him with the online purchase, which included the Bigfoot and a few other small items.

As the kids made their final preparations for the haunted woods, they remembered that it would probably help if they actually invited some guests. Crystal and Freddie collaborated on a computer-generated invitation flyer that they could hand out to a limited number of local families with little kids.

In addition to providing the requisite who/what/where/when information on the invitation, Freddie said he wanted to add one final spicy detail to the end of the haunted woods flyer: a reference to a Sasquatch attraction. Crystal wasn't certain the Sasquatch reference was a great idea.

"Are you sure you want to mention a Sasquatch?" Crystal asked Freddie. "The spiders, the ghouls, the Dork Dracula—we'll have all that stuff. But Sasquatch? Are we suggesting we're going to…show him?"

Freddie considered the question. "It's not who you think. We actually will have a Sasquatch as long as my cardboard creature ships in time to get here for Halloween," he said.

Crystal seemed satisfied with the explanation. "Well, I guess that's okay," she said.

Come to the annual Pine View Street haunted house – this time in the scary woods!

When: Saturday, October 30 at 7 p.m.
Where: Freddy and Crystal's house (where else?)
What: A tour of the haunted woods that you'll never forget!
Why: Because it's Halloween. Duh!

Come and see...

- Huge monster spiders
- The famous haunted toilet
- Flying ghouls aplenty
- Dork Dracula
- T-Rex (uh, no, we don't have a T-Rex)
- Sasquatch (yes!)

About a week before Halloween, Crystal and Freddie went around the neighborhood and left invitation flyers at the nearby houses where they knew kids lived. Although they had invited the Mentons in past years, Crystal and Freddie were quite hesitant to invite the family of the infamous Mikey to the haunted woods. They ended up doing so only because of the closeness of the Menton house to the McKenzie house, and the fact that

Mikey had a nice little sister, Jane. Crystal and Freddie secretly hoped that perhaps Mikey would have something else planned for Halloween night— perhaps toilet papering City Hall or leading a pack of feral hogs through a shopping center.

In addition to inviting the usual group of neighborhood families, Freddie had one additional special guest in mind. The day after the kids finished the flyers, Freddie took one in to school and gave it to his science teacher, Mr. Milanovich. He remembered the teacher saying that he had two young children, and Freddie thought the kid-oriented attractions, not to mention the Sasquatch reference, might spur Mr. Milanovich to drive over with his family and give the haunted woods a try.

By Saturday afternoon, virtually everything was in place for the haunted woods. Crystal and Freddie, with the help of a few of their dad's tall ladders, tethered all the ghouls, ghosts and flying mummies up in trees and readied them for swinging action. Lots of big candles had been placed on the ground throughout the tour route; the kids would light them and thus have a nicely lit path through the woods. A few candles were placed up in the crooks of old trees to add extra effect. The spider sleds were strategically positioned so that the person not conducting the tour at that moment could grab the fishing wire and pull the spider along the ground to deliver the big arachnid attack. Crystal set up the music player to emit an extended series of Halloween sound effects: quavering moans, ghastly shrieking, strange organ music, grinding chains, spooky cat meows and the like. Crystal and Freddie would soon lead the families along the route one by one. The entire circuit only took a few minutes to complete, so families wouldn't have to wait too long at the entrance for their turn at the tour.

By dinnertime that day, all was ready. Crystal and Freddie were nervous but excited. Now they just had to wait for nightfall and the witching hour to arrive.

6 – HAUNTING

Early one evening, the two small humans were seen just inside the tree line busying themselves lighting small fire holders and triggering slightly disturbing sounds from a small sonic device. Groups of other humans began appearing at the edge of the forest—apparently both parents and children in the species. They appeared to be awaiting entry to the strange display that the two small humans had erected. The boy and girl began leading the groups one by one along a predefined path. One small human would serve as the guide, while the other would leap out or otherwise attempt to frighten the families with a contraption. Then the two humans would switch roles, repeatedly. They duplicated the same series of actions with each family. It was very strange. Most of the human visitors to the woods seemed agreeable and rather amused by the proceedings, while other individuals behaved badly and required forceful scolding.

The first families started showing up at the McKenzie's just after 7 on Saturday night. A family or two walked up the long driveway and the sidewalk to ring the doorbell, and were greeted by Mrs. or Mr. McKenzie, who redirected them around the back of the house. The other families just followed Crystal and Freddie's crude signs that pointed them to the back yard.

This way to the

Pine View Street

Haunted Woods

Moms, dads and kids walked across the back yard to the very edge of the woods and stopped under a hanging sign that said, "Haunting Victims Wait Here."

The Dyer family was the first to go through the scary circuit, with two little girls age ten and under providing the scream energy as they made their way along the guided path. Crystal was happy that the Dyers had gone first; daughters Jenny and Abigail set a resounding example with their high-pitched screams echoing through the forest. The waiting guests figured they might just be in for a hefty haunting.

While the mechanical spooks always got a curious and slightly mystified response from the guests, it was when the ghouls, ghosts or vampires leapt out from behind trees or from coffins that the screams really got going. Invariably the youngest of the guests would begin holding onto their parents' hands for dear life as they walked along, and the amused parents would serve as temporary shields if the little ones needed somewhere to hide when a werewolf or Dork Dracula sprung out.

At one point Crystal was pulling a big spider along on its forest sled toward the Menton family, when the sled banged into little Jane Menton and the spider fell off. There was an uncomfortable few seconds of silence as everyone looked down and assessed the unusual situation. Improvising, Freddie came rushing madly out from behind a tree waving his arms and moaning, "Beware the killer spiders. They will surely eat your legs if you touch them!" With that he ran up to the Mentons, scooped up the stranded spider and sled, and ran back behind a tree to prepare for his next scare.

A bit later as the Smyth family was coming through, Crystal took her designated position behind a tree where she would unhook the harness line to a big hanging ghost figure that the kids had bought at the Halloween store. It hung from fishing wire around its neck, which would have been a most uncomfortable arrangement had it been a still-living being. But this time, as the ghost came swinging down toward the family, the vertical suspension line untied and the ghost took a clumsy flop onto the forest floor. The Smyths all got a good laugh as the now flattened phantom ended its creepy career in a heap atop the leaves. Both host kids observed the crash of the swinging ghost and realized they'd probably have to do without him for the rest of the night, since there wouldn't be an opportunity to climb back up and reset the high suspension line.

Freddie's favorite part of the spook fest was the very end of the tour, when he could play the role of Bigfoot. As Crystal led each family toward the exit sign at the edge of the woods, Freddie would vault out from behind a tree, holding his large cardboard Bigfoot cutout in front of him and growling for everything he was worth. This almost always resulted in a final scream from the little ones and their parents, which set the scene especially well for the next set of guests to enter. In fact, with the exit sign visible, some of the small kids ran right out of the woods screaming upon Freddie's fearsome advance and monstrous roar.

So, as it turns out, Freddie's contribution to the kids' invitation flyer was in fact right on: a Sasquatch was indeed part of their show, even if it was of the cardboard variety.

As Crystal began leading one of the later families into the woods, Freddie noticed that it was Mr. Milanovich, his wife and his two young children. Seeing this, Freddie was positively gleeful that Mr. Milanovich had accepted the invitation and brought his unsuspecting family to the ghoulish grounds. Freddie scrunched down inside his Dracula coffin and prepared to unleash a full-scale scare.

From the coffin, Freddie soon heard the cue words from Crystal. ("And in this dark place, all manner of evil creatures await you.") Freddie knew the family would be standing right in front of the coffin now. He slowly slid the big plywood lid aside and stood up, stretching both arms up and out to the side as far as he could so his big black cape would hang down menacingly. A candle in front of the coffin provided some spooky upward illumination of Dork Dracula's face. He looked down at Mr. Milanovich's kids—a small boy and an even smaller girl—and bared his fangs, saying, "I vant to drink your BLOOD!" Each wide-eyed child emitted a quick little scream and instinctively ran behind his or her mother's legs for protection.

Composed and wry as usual, the smiling Mr. Milanovich just rubbed his chin as he observed Freddie and said, "Well well, Transylvanian hijinks right here in Cherryville."

Freddie couldn't let his teacher off that easy without trying to instill some additional fear.

"I am *the undead*!" began Freddie in a more threatening tone than that of his initial volley, "and I will take your life with my fury."

The teacher considered this threat.

"I don't think so," began Mr. Milanovich, calmly. "I just think you're pretty washed out and green because you had the fish surprise for lunch at school yesterday, Mr. Drac."

"Ha!" shouted Freddie back at his teacher. Freddie's reaction was a laugh as much as anything. He did his best to counter quickly. "I am never surprised by fish, and…and when I turn into a bat I will pursue you and your loved ones as you make your way home tonight!"

Mr. Milanovich was no more fearful of this threat than any of the others, but this time he went along.

"Alright, mister bat boy," said the teacher, "We'll keep our eyes open for winged rats and sixth graders—which are pretty much the same thing anyway."

Crystal didn't quite know what to make of this ongoing, unusual exchange, and after tolerating some delay she got the family's attention and led them toward the next scare.

The remainder of the scares directed at the Milanovich family went well, and upon nearing the end of the haunted trail, they got the full dose of Sasquatch attack. Freddie burst out from behind the tree wielding his cardboard Bigfoot alter ego, and roared at his teacher's family with considerable bombast. The little ones screamed very loudly, and the parents led them toward the exit sign.

As the Milanovichs were getting ready to leave, Freddie and Crystal saw that there was only one more party awaiting the tour of terror. It was Mikey Menton along with three of his pals from the neighborhood and the surrounding area. Mikey hadn't walked with his parents when they came through the woods with little Jane, so Mikey and his minions were now unmoored from the moderating influence of adults. It wasn't a particularly encouraging scene...

As Crystal started the tour and began leading the boys around, she immediately realized that she would not be getting the same caliber of reaction from these boys as she had from the families before them. It began with Freddie's emergence from the coffin, when Mikey took one look at Freddie and blurted out, "Hey look, it's Jerk Dorkula!" The other boys roared with laughter. Freddie didn't even get a chance to deliver his signature line about wanting to drink the blood of the guests, though at this point he would certainly like to have taken a hefty bite out of the brutes.

And as Freddie and Crystal had seen time and again at the bus stop and at school, once the Mikey Menton train got rolling, it was awfully hard to apply the brakes.

A bit later when it was Crystal's turn to execute the scare—via the haunted toilet sitting atop a big backless cardboard box—Mikey grabbed her hand and yanked it when she put it up through the box and the toilet seat.

"Ow, you stupid...!" Crystal reacted with shock.

Various snickers and giggles ensued.

Coming up to the spot where the flying ghost had previously held sway, one of the Menton minions, Tom DeStefano, scooped up the now grounded ghoul and roughly tossed its limp corpse headfirst off the lit trail and out into the dark of the woods. Again, the other boys had some laughs at this.

Could this rude gesture have triggered some unknowable response on the part of the forest?

When it was time for the spider scare, Crystal pulled on the line and got the sled disc going speedily across the leaves. But Mikey saw it coming and stuck out one of his feet to obstruct the spider's advance. The spider and sled banged into his leg, somewhat as it did to his sister earlier. However, Mikey snatched up the furry dark spider and savagely crumpled a few of its long legs, and like Tom with the ghost before him, tossed the creature off the trail in a ruined pile in the dark.

This action was also apparently not unnoticed.

"Hey!" yelled Freddie at Mikey. "You didn't need to do that."

"Oh yes I did," replied Mikey. "I was SO scared." The other boys snickered compliantly.

Although they had not communicated it in words, Crystal and Freddie were both surely thinking it would be good to just dispense with additional scares and get the unwelcome guests out of the woods without further ado.

The big boys' fun had seemingly reached a fever pitch by the time they approached the final scare and the exit. They were laughing and occasionally pushing each other randomly as their trundle through the terrors was closing up. Now it was time for Freddie's Sasquatch to appear and do its climactic thing.

Though he would rather have been undergoing a painful dental procedure at that moment, Freddie dutifully leapt out from the tree and delivered a halfhearted roar from behind his cardboard creature.

"Hrrrr!" he growled with minimal enthusiasm.

"Whoa, guys, look: it's little-foot!" yelled Mikey to the others.

Two of the boys, Darian Morse and Jim Doyle, issued rasping giggles at the sight of the less-than-imposing cardboard monster. Tom DeStefano was compelled to comment further.

"What's that you're hidin' behind, Freddie, an overgrown pizza box?!"

The other three boys all laughed heartily in response.

With mob mirth having reached its peak and with Freddie only a few feet in front of the boys, Mikey stepped up and, as he usually did, crossed the proverbial line. He walked quickly up to Freddie and grabbed the Sasquatch figure, with Freddie still holding onto it with both hands. Mikey gave the cardboard Sasquatch and Freddie a very violent shove backward.

Falling, Freddie let go of the Sasquatch figure in mid-tumble. He fell flat on his back in the leaves, stunned. He could only grunt out, "Ooomph!" as he hit the ground with a hard thud, the wind instantly knocked out of him. The rigid monster landed ungracefully on top of him.

This triggered a crashing wave of laughter from the boys. A couple of them pointed at the inert creature and Freddie, grabbing at their own sides with the force of their cackling.

From over near the exit area, Crystal saw Freddie get slammed to the ground by the much larger Mikey Menton. She was about to run over to Freddie when something in the air very rapidly changed and stopped her in her tracks.

At that very moment, Mikey, Tom and the other two boys turned around from Freddie to head victoriously for the exit. But as they did so, their progress was immediately stopped by something unexpected right in front of them.

It was a huge, dark figure standing directly between the boys and the trail exit. Each boy tilted his head back and looked up in shock and wonderment at the figure. The boys' raucous guffaws were instantly replaced by absolute stunned silence. Nothing moved or made a sound.

Frozen, the boys each tried to quickly figure out what they were seeing. Some sort of dark creature of incomparable size was blocking their forest exit. At first Mikey thought that perhaps Crystal was pulling some sort of closing stunt, hiding behind an even bigger cardboard monster shape than the one Freddie had used earlier. But a moment later, as Crystal was making her way over to check on Freddie amidst the commotion, all the boys saw her at the same time. With Freddie and Crystal standing together, this third figure had to be something else entirely. It was apparently…a *real* monster.

As this realization instantly sunk into the boys, Mikey Menton uttered by far the most intelligent response that the boys could muster at this moment, only saying, "What the….?!"

The large figure's intent, to this point uncertain, soon became crystal clear. It took one step forward toward Mikey, clenched its huge fists downward, and let fly an impossibly deep, angry roar lasting several seconds, shattering the stillness of the woods and blasting the boys with a rush of foul air. Each of the boys reacted as if punched violently in the stomach; Tom and Darian actually dropped to their knees at the sound. The roar rocketed throughout the forest, even stopping Mr. Milanovich and his family in their tracks as they were nearing their car quite some distance away on Pine View Street.

As did anyone who had ever encountered even the remotest trace of the Sasquatch's energy, the boys' brains switched from attempting to understand their situation, to abject fear that their lives were about to be violently and rapidly extinguished. Each boy unconsciously soiled his pants at this experience of primal terror. (The Sasquatch may or may not have realized that wet-pants-syndrome was becoming more and more common in this little corner of Oregon.)

With the Sasquatch still menacingly standing in place at the trail exit, one by one the boys bolted and started to run far to either side of the creature and toward the lights of the McKenzie house. All four boys screamed at the top of their lungs as they ran, waving their arms and batting their way through the brush. Freddie had always marveled at the sharp, high-pitched shrieks that little girls could emit when they screamed and played. But little girls had nothing on the sound of the four hapless, frightened neighborhood urchins hurtling through the dark forest toward the imagined safety of their mothers' grasps, almost certain never to return to this spot again.

Finally, for the first time on this long, trying day, Crystal and Freddie stopped what they were doing and looked at each other deeply for several seconds. Then, simultaneously, they broke down into peals of untamed, belly-busting laughter. All of the tension and disappointment of the day instantly dissolved into delirious delight.

Their huge Halloween partner simply stood still and took in the tattered remnants of the haunted woods and the peculiar extremes of human behavior and emotion observed in this strangest of places tonight.

7 – BURNING

The rather unexplainable night forest display had come to a close. Groups of humans left the woods one by one after their experience of the odd performance by the two young individuals. Several young males deserved and received some punishment. But now something was going terribly wrong in the woods. A natural threat had appeared that was no friend to creatures—human or otherwise. The dangerous situation represented a risk to the physical environment, and potentially to the lives and belongings of creatures within it.

Although it had not seemed so at a number of points during the night, the haunted woods ended up being quite a success for Crystal and Freddie. Certainly there were occasional technical glitches associated with the spooky contraptions, but everyone seemed to enjoy the show in the end. Those who ended up *not* enjoying the show (instead, having to flee) would just have to get over it, if they could.

Crystal and Freddie lingered at the exit for several minutes to review and laugh over a number of things that had happened during their tours of terror—particularly the flight of the buffoons at the end. In the morning they would need to return to the woods and begin the laborious process of cleaning up the many items of theatrical debris now littering the landscape.

The kids didn't particularly notice that the Bigfoot had gradually backed off into the shadows after all the hubbub and was again at a distance.

"Well, that was a heck of a lot of work," commented Freddie, "but it was worth it just to see Mikey and his buds get the bejeebers scared out of them," he said.

Crystal replied, "Yeah, and I think most of the little kids really liked it, though we may want to reevaluate our flying ghost when we do this next year."

"Right. A few of these guys didn't hold up so well once the show went on," Freddie added, also considering the crumpled giant spider, and to some extent the cardboard Bigfoot figure.

Mr. Milanovich had returned from his car to check on the kids after the very loud, angry roar that he and everyone in the vicinity had heard just after the woodsy show ended. Mr. Milanovich walked up and met the kids at the entrance/exit point.

"Um, can you guys identify the origin of that... sound?" he asked Crystal and Freddie.

The kids looked at each other knowingly and didn't respond for several seconds.

"Well," started Freddie, "you remember our big backwoods guest that I referred to? He was here with us tonight."

"So, that wasn't the cardboard Bigfoot asserting itself—it was your...real Bigfoot pal?" he asked.

"That's right," said Freddie. "We said on the invitation that we had a Sasquatch in our show, and even though you didn't really see him, boy was he here."

Mr. Milanovich thought about that for a moment. "Uh, was he particularly upset about something tonight?" he asked tentatively. "Whatever the sound was that he made was not exactly a mating call."

Crystal replied, "Let's just say that Mikey Menton's bunch got under his skin a little bit, and he didn't hold back telling them about it."

"Wow. But I guess I shouldn't be surprised," continued Mr. Milanovich. "Mr. Menton has all the charm of a pack of fire ants in the pants."

The kids giggled at that.

"And speaking of fire," started Mr. Milanovich, "are you guys aware that there's smoke coming from the back of your woods?"

He casually pointed toward the rear of the trail, in the direction of the kids' fort. There was indeed a lot of smoke, and some flames, visible in that direction.

"Oh no!" cried Crystal.

Apparently the candle in the crook of a hollowed out tree had ignited the long-dead innards of that tree. Another candle at the edge of the trail, sitting next to some tall, dried weeds and a small leaf pile, had lit the surrounding brush aflame as the candle burned lower and lower throughout the night.

Once they realized what was happening, Crystal and Freddie both bolted toward the back of the woods to check out the scene, with Mr. Milanovich trailing closely behind. When they got close to the tree from which the flying ghost had swung, they saw that the fire was getting pretty far along. Smoke was billowing out of the hollow in the old tree containing the candle. Flames were climbing what was left of the tree, probably reaching up 15 or 20 feet.

Nearby, another fire was spreading horizontally across the leaves and weeds at the edge of the trail. As the kids got close they realized that this fire had the potential to spread, and spread fast.

"Geez, what do we do?" yelled Freddie to Crystal.

"I don't know," she answered. "Maybe we can get a fire extinguisher from back at the house or something," she added.

"I think you're going to need some help with this," chimed in Mr. Milanovich from behind Crystal and Freddie. Usually he was fully unflappable, but right now he wasn't sounding witty or clever. He was concerned.

Just then Freddie's mom and dad appeared at the woods, rushing out to meet the kids after smelling smoke and getting worried.

"How did this happen?" asked Mrs. McKenzie in a panicked tone, quite out of breath.

No one said anything at first.

"There are lots of candles here," replied Mr. Milanovich as he scanned the area. "And some of them are still burning."

Looking around, the kids both realized they had made a mistake not watching the candles more closely. Attending to all the candles scattered across the woods that busy night didn't quite rate at the top of the kids' list of priorities. What was up until now a fanciful, very creative holiday display had taken a serious turn.

"I'm going to call 911," said Crystal's mom hurriedly. She pulled her phone out of her pocket and did just that, stepping away several paces as she placed the call. She provided the address to the dispatcher and described the unusual situation of there being a fire in the woods behind the family's house. She did not bother to mention the spook-related specifics of the situation.

Mr. McKenzie and Mr. Milanovich moved toward the fires to see if there was anything they could do. At this point, there wasn't much.

"I have no way to put out these fires," said a flustered Mr. McKenzie as he got right up to the edge of the brush fire. Without a shovel, a nearby stream of water or a fire extinguisher, he resorted to just stomping on some of the smaller flames around the edges of the fire. His efforts at putting out the fire were about as successful as Mikey Menton trying to remain quiet in church.

Crystal and Freddie stood rather helplessly in the background watching the flames build while their father played a hapless dancing game of hot-foot with the flames. Like the kids, Mr. Milanovich could only stand and watch as things got worse.

After several minutes the group could hear the advance of sirens. Help was on the way. But of course the sound served to deepen Crystal and Freddie' sinking feeling, as it was painfully clear that the remains of their show now needed a public safety response.

Two firefighters soon appeared at the edge of the woods and jogged up the trail leading to where the people were standing in front of the flames.

Without introductory fanfare, each firefighter moved toward one of the fires—one, to the brush fire at the back, and the other to the fire in the old tree toward the right side of the woods. One firefighter pulled out a walkie-talkie to communicate with others back at the trucks.

Looking up curiously into the trees in the immediate area, the other firefighter said to whoever might be listening, "Uh, you all know there's a mummy up in that tree."

At any other time the comment would have been highly amusing. Tonight, no one could muster a response to the statement.

A few minutes later, a well-equipped fire jeep drove through the back of the McKenzie's yard and up to the edge of the woods. It stopped for a moment then drove right through the brush and into the woods, weaving between trees as it headed for the fires. The small white truck had a large spindle of fire hose in its open back. The high beam headlights of the truck lit pretty much everything in the vicinity.

The vehicle-based firefighters reached the tree fire first, since the second fire was further back in the woods. Upon getting the truck to the first fire, the crew unwound the hose and started spraying down the flames on the old tree with water from the truck's onboard tank.

The men got the tree fire under control pretty quickly, since to this point it was confined to just the vertical space of the single old tree. But moving with the truck to the more widespread brush fire at the back of the woods, the firefighters' work took a bit longer.

All of the McKenzies and Mr. Milanovich moved closer to the brush fire to watch the firefighters work. The three men, one of whom was using a fire axe and a shovel, had very nearly gotten the last of the fire out at the back of the haunted woods, when everyone noticed something odd right at the edge of where Crystal and Freddie's fort was situated.

Someone was stepping out from behind the fort into the direct view of all the firefighters and onlookers. It was the Bigfoot.

The creature was holding some items apparently pulled from the fort. It had Freddie's bat in one hand and Crystal's guitar in the other. The items looked to be about the size of paper clips in the hands of the huge creature. Perhaps the creature was trying to save the items from the flames. Who could be sure?

Realizing what they were seeing, Crystal and Freddie both felt a warm rush of emotion. Soon a tear appeared at the corner of Crystal's eye. This wasn't because of the smoke in the air.

Upon seeing everyone in front of it, the creature stopped still. It stood in place observing the small crowd of six totally stunned humans, and two familiar ones. The young firefighter who was manning the hose had turned it off and stood with mouth agape, staring awestruck at the creature.

"Oh my God," whispered Mrs. McKenzie, to the others, at the sight.

The older firefighter with the hand-held equipment said, "What in God's *name*...?!" His voice trailed off, as he was fully unable to complete his sentence. He dropped his hardware with a clang.

"Freddie, your accounts of this individual were spot on," said Mr. Milanovich, quietly.

After that statement, no one could summon any further words. The huge figure simply stood right in front of them, lit indirectly by the truck headlights, apparently just as stunned as the people were.

Soon the creature looked to its left toward where Crystal and Freddie were standing. It bent down and very gently laid down the bat and guitar salvaged from the fort. It stood up again to its full height but kept its gaze on the kids. Crystal and Freddie were quite aware of how the creature seemed to focus on them, and in a rather intense way.

The stillness and quiet in the forest now held sway over everyone, along with the misty cloud of slowly clearing smoke.

The creature then turned quickly to its right and strode away into the woods. The crunching of leaves beneath the creature was the first sound anyone had heard in several minutes. That sound didn't last long as, after a few fleeting seconds in sight, the creature assumed its customary speed of travel through the forest and was, very quickly, completely gone.

The humans remained stock still in a flabbergasted group, astounded at what they had just witnessed amidst the smoky mystery of this evening.

Crystal and Freddie experienced a mixed jumble of feelings as their friend disappeared this time.

8 - AFTERMATH

The unfortunate fiery incident in the woods, and the sizeable number of humans that attended to it, changed the dynamic in the area. Many individuals at once had borne witness to the previously unknown giant of the forest. A balance had been upset. Although limited contact with the two young humans seemed to still have value, the close interaction with many other individuals during the fire-scorched night could prove problematic. Other, more remote regions might better sustain a solitary life in the woods.

It did not take long for the story of the haunted woods fire and the Bigfoot to make its way beyond the confines of Pine View Street. Given the involvement of county employees in the Halloween night fire, official reports were submitted, which soon resulted in the story making it to attention of the Cherryville Times newspaper. A small article appeared in the local news section of the paper several days later.

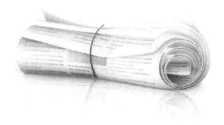

Soon many residents of Cherryville and the surrounding area learned about the incredible Halloween Bigfoot sighting. At coffee shops, hair salons and grocery stores, folks were abuzz over the latest and perhaps most dramatic in the long line of reported encounters with Sasquatch in the area. The involvement of a number of children in the encounter—as opposed to some adult back-country hikers or woodsmen—lent an extra element of drama to the incident. And the fact that several county firefighters on an official call saw the Bigfoot, in addition to a teacher, and Freddie and Crystal's parents, added credibility to the eyewitness accounts. The event was clearly no Halloween hoax or backwoods boast.

And of course, news of the oddball adventure spread quickly at Freddie and Crystal's school. All the kids at Monroe Middle soon learned about the appearance of the Bigfoot. Crystal or Freddie would get stopped in the hall once in a while as curious classmates peppered them with all sorts of questions about the encounter. Both of the McKenzie kids did their best to give accurate, low-key answers to the often off-kilter questions.

As a witness to the Bigfoot appearance, Mr. Milanovich was certainly an authority when it came to describing what everyone saw. But in Earth Science class on Monday, Mr. Milanovich generously gave Freddie the opportunity to recount the full scope of the adventure for the class. Freddie stood somewhat uncomfortably in front of the chalkboard at the head of the class and told the whole story, from the time of the kids' first encounter with the creature through the bizarre events of Saturday night. Freddie's classmates sat in rare rapt attention as he told the tale.

As was happening at times out in the halls at school, some ungraceful questions were lobbed in Freddie's direction in Earth Science class.

"Why didn't you shoot the creature?" asked John Gresham bluntly.

"There was no reason to shoot it," replied Freddie with exasperation.

John pressed on. "But weren't you scared?!" he asked.

"No, not at all. We've been seeing the creature for a while and we're pretty used to him by now," Freddie explained.

The full import of that response struck John pretty solidly. He could only respond, "Wow."

Sara Jones asked a more pertinent question. "Where do you think he went after Saturday night?"

Freddie had to think for a few seconds to come up with a response. "Well, I'm not sure," he began, "but I think he lives pretty far out in the woods, so he probably went somewhere out there where there aren't any fires right now."

Until this point, Freddie hadn't taken much time to think about the Bigfoot's reaction to the craziness of Saturday night, but Sara's question elevated his sense of uncertainty about the creature's current welfare and location.

A small subset of students was not at all interested in the creature's welfare. Instead, they busied themselves with face-saving, rather dishonest efforts to report the events of Saturday night. Specifically, it was Mikey Menton's minions who made no attempt to present an accurate recounting.

In their retelling of the incident, the boys were soon reporting that they had faced the creature bravely.

"I could have taken that thing," bragged Darian Morse at the lunch table on Monday.

But in fact, Darian and his highly moistened pants made one of the hastiest retreats of all the terrified boys that night. He was long gone by the time Freddy and Crystal got their laugh at the boys' expense.

Mikey himself also strongly shaded his account of the events in order to position himself in a better light. "I was going to stay and trash that dumb Bigfoot," he reported to some friends, "but the haunted woods thing was too uncool for me to hang around."

He hoped his omission of more specific details would serve to deflect any additional scrutiny.

Some of the boys reported to other Monroe students that the creature was nine feet tall. Tom DeStefano said it was ten feet tall. Jim Doyle estimated that it was closer to twelve.

The rising tide of misinformation was matched only by the consistent admiration with which everyone else was treating Freddie and Crystal around school.

With three key witnesses to the newsworthy events being part of the Monroe Middle population, the larger school community seemed to enjoy being somewhat at the epicenter of the soon-to-be-legend story.

Before long, life settled down a bit and got back to its normal, rather mundane pace for everyone involved.

Over the course of several weeks, Freddie and Crystal's parents questioned them about various points of their "relationship" with the Sasquatch. Parental agreement quickly moved in the direction of encouraging the kids not to go back into the woods for further contact with the creature.

At dinner one night, Mrs. McKenzie said, "You know, that thing could really harm you. You never know what it could do. It's not a person. It's a very wild animal, and a very big, strong animal. I don't think you two should be out there again."

Freddie and Crystal sat silently, mulling this warning.

Crystal eventually said, "It had every chance to hurt us—a whole bunch of times. And it chose not to. Then on Saturday night, it was pretty clearly standing up for Freddie," she asserted. "Plus it saved some of our stuff from the fire," she added.

"That may be," said Dad, "but logic tells you that it's just not safe to be out there unprotected with a huge wild animal. A bear in a zoo could seem friendly for a few minutes, but when its instincts kick in, it could end you quickly," he said.

"The creature would never 'end' us," said Freddy, forcefully. "It's so much more than a wild animal. It understands us. It's a little bit like...our friend."

There. Someone had said it. It was the first acknowledgement in front of Mom and Dad that the bond between Bigfoot, boy and girl was something quite rare and special. At least at this sitting, Mr. and Mrs. McKenzie didn't press their case.

The parents' warnings were never really put to the test, though. The impact of the fire and the close brush with a number of witnesses seemed to have changed the creature's behavior. It apparently wasn't in the area now.

Crystal and Freddie spent most of their free time in the woods during the available daylight hours of chilly early November. On the surface they were focused on cleaning up the scattered remnants of the haunted woods. But their actual agenda involved using their powers of observation to discern whether the Bigfoot had returned at any point. They kept a keen eye out for footprints and tree structures. They strained their ears listening for sounds. They stayed alert for the possible return of Sasquatch smells.

Their cleanup efforts took on an increasingly unhurried pace. However, throughout this time, the kids' forays to the woods did not result in any signs of the creature's presence.

Freddie had his bat again, and during their cleanup trips and other visits to the fort he would occasionally make some loud wood knocks, hoping for a response from the creature. But unlike prior attempts at contact, there was nothing but silence after Freddie's tree knocks now. Crystal took a few swings as well but got the same lonely, empty result.

After pulling down the last of the haunted woods décor—the wayward, tree-bound mummy that the firefighter had commented about—there was nothing left in the area but a large, charred tree and some blackened brush near the kids' fort.

A couple of months after the fire, Freddie was out on the back patio of the house one night with his dog Marty. He thought he heard the signature long howl of the Bigfoot from a great distance, but he wasn't sure. This was the only instance of potential evidence of the creature's presence in the region during the months after the haunted woods events. Whatever the creature was doing now, it was clearly not in any way nearby.

As all events do, the Halloween haunted woods adventure soon started slipping into the past. Life had fully returned to normal on Pine View Street and beyond. The brush with Bigfoot settled into the fabric of local lore, and the creature was not seen in the area again.

A young boy and girl had experienced a positive, unexpected instance of small-town celebrity, but their sense of disappointment at losing touch with their forest friend clouded many of their other experiences during this time in their lives.

9 - MIGRATION

Seasons came and went. As weather changed and food source populations moved about the wilderness, it was best to follow the natural flow of these conditions. In the interest of getting adequate nourishment and having minimal human contact, it didn't make sense to stay in any one place too long. The huge expanses of wilderness in the Northwest made it possible to remain virtually unseen and undisturbed. Large, mysterious primates were observed in the region on extremely rare occasions, but as usual, they managed to remain elusive.

Over time, Freddie and Crystal's lives became much more like the lives of all the other kids in the area.

Crystal continued pursuing her passion for music, and for artistic expression in general. She acted in drama productions in high school, and particularly enjoyed musicals where she could sing in addition to acting. Both her music and language skills moved forward in great strides, and it was clear she would pursue a path in the arts or a similar field of communication.

She continued to write songs, performing them solo at school functions where she accompanied herself on acoustic guitar. In time she even got some gigs out in the community, using the singer/songwriter format. She performed locally in coffee shops, at craft fairs and at charity events.

One of Crystal's favorite funny compositions was a tune called Bigfoot Love where she imagined a large male Bigfoot courting a female mate in the woods. ("It looked like Sasquatch, yes indeed / finding romance in the weeds.") The song always garnered ample giggles when she performed it. It was the only piece in her song catalog that paid homage to her Sasquatch experience years ago as a middle school student. Beneath the fun aspect of the song, though, was a wistful memory of the music's living subject.

Freddie's interests took on a rather scientific bent as his unique encounter with a mysterious life form, plus the bond he shared with Mr. Milanovich regarding the creature, motivated his interest in zoological pursuits. He enjoyed his studies in biology, and he even looked into cryptozoology—studying animals whose existence has not yet been proven. Like many before him, Freddie's encounter with something that couldn't be fully explained spurred a lifetime interest in studying the clues and reports of the creature across the region and beyond.

And like his father, Freddie continued to follow the fluctuating fortunes of his favorite sports teams. The Seattle Seahawks and Mariners only rarely rose to the heights of national eminence, but Freddie remained a loyal fan regardless.

After graduation from high school, Crystal attended Southern Oregon University to study theater. She succeeded rather well in making the transition from living at home to dorm life on campus. In addition to her studies, she continued to do coffee house-type performances of her music whenever she could, and she earned extra money working as a waitress at various restaurants in Ashland.

Freddie had good academic success throughout high school. He maintained a small group of friends (including the previously sign-smashed Trevor Weldon) with whom he could have a pretty good time. Fairly common were online group video game competitions and outings to the local theaters where the boys took in the favored sci-fi and action films of the day.

All during high school, Freddie tried to keep some distance from the always absurd Mikey Menton, whose exploits had only temporarily been subdued by his humbling encounter with the massive forest creature.

Odd deeds for which Mikey gained infamy in high school included eating seven Big Mac sandwiches at a sitting after a football game. He and his minions also climbed a local water storage tower late one summer night and went for a swim—smack in the middle of the community's water supply. Another time he and his pals amassed a number of buckets of paint, running up and attacking a kiddy float in the Harvest Days parade in town and drenching the unsuspecting little float pixies with hideous splashes of blue.

Mikey seemed well on his way to realizing at least one of his stated career goals: he wanted to be either a competitive eater or an industrial demolition expert, or maybe even a monster truck driver—anything where an act of high wackiness could generate maximum attention. Clearly Mikey did not go quietly as young life unfolded.

10 - REUNION

Around the time of summer solstice, the earth was warm as the planet's orbit positioned it to face the sun more directly. In the early summer, food was plentiful in the deep forest. The rains of spring had filled the landscape with lushness everywhere. The rivers ran full. Young creatures took their first steps upon the earth. Sunlight filtered down through the tall trees and nourished the green expanse of plant life in every direction. Given the passage of time, ground that had been left some years ago no longer bore a human footprint nor represented territory to be avoided. Although it isn't possible to return in time to prior placements of individuals in the unique orbits of their lives, every so often, worlds come back into contact as their orbits overlap.

After two years living away at college, it was time for Crystal to return to the family home in Cherryville. She had finished her second spring semester at Southern Oregon U., and now it was time for a family celebration of Freddie's graduation from high school.

Mr. and Mrs. McKenzie's relatives from around the region, plus some of Freddie's school and neighborhood friends, arrived for a cookout late on a bright, sunny Saturday afternoon in early June. Mr. McKenzie cooked burgers and hot dogs on the grill, and there were plenty of refreshments for the twenty or so guests who milled about the McKenzie back yard in front of the glorious back wall of big trees. Mrs. McKenzie was happy both about Freddie's graduation and the fact that Crystal was back for the summer and could share some of her talents and charm with the family.

On the back patio, Crystal set up the equipment that she typically used for her solo music gigs. She got out her acoustic guitar, plugged a microphone into a small amplifier and serenaded the crowd with some of her original tunes (including Bigfoot Love), plus a few folk-type standards. Eating and drinking as they wandered and socialized around the back yard, the relatives and friends got a kick out of the gentle yet very inventive and original music Crystal was providing. Freddie and some of his pals, however, were less than impressed with the entertainment. Most of the boys would have preferred some good hard heavy metal or rap.

After 40 minutes or so of playing and singing, Crystal took a break to get a soda and cool off. A few relatives came up to her to compliment her. Meanwhile Freddie and some of his friends were playing Frisbee beside the house.

After absorbing the family's compliments, Crystal wandered over to where the boys' Frisbee game appeared to be breaking up. She hadn't spent much time with Freddie during this fun but hectic day, and she hoped to chat a bit. Trevor and a couple of other boys were moving toward the middle of the back yard to grab some refreshments from a cooler. This left Crystal and Freddie alone for a few minutes.

"So, you're the big man now, ready to take on the world," Crystal said with a bit of sarcastic drama.

"Well, not really," began Freddie, "but I'm at least ready to take on the status of non-high-schooler. Senior year was pretty much a waste of time," he said.

"Yeah, I remember mostly phoning it in during senior year," Crystal said, "although I did enjoy acting in the Little Shop of Horrors play and then the talent show toward the end of the year."

"Oh, geez," sighed Freddie, having been brought back to thoughts of Crystal's music. "Talent is one thing, but...Bigfoot Love? 'Finding romance in the weeds'?! How much more can you butcher that topic for your own gain?"

"For my own gain?" Crystal asked with a huff. "I'm having fun with something that used to mean a lot to us," she explained.

Freddie asked, "So you honor the topic by making a foolish public presentation of it?"

"It's fun, not foolish," Crystal retorted. By this point the lightness was starting to drain a little bit from the kids' conversation, much as it often did many years ago.

"Okay then, it's fun," said Freddie, "but it also kind of sucks."

Crystal took a sharp intake of breath at Freddie's less-than-tender statement.

"I'd like to see you try to write something," Crystal resumed. "You've still got your eyeballs stuck to those dumb video games where you can just hide in front of the screen and accomplish nothing at all," she said.

"Well, at least I prefer not to make an idiot of myself out in public," said Freddie stoutly.

To the kids' shock, just as Freddie finished his statement, they saw a shadow pass over their heads, and less than a second later a large branch crashed loudly against the side of the house right next to them, and dropped to the ground. A few of the party guests around the corner heard the crash and looked around to see what happened.

Crystal and Freddie were jolted into silence at the totally unexpected event. After recoiling downward in response to the huge crash, they looked at each other with eyes wide. Could this really be happening?

Still stooped over, the kids both looked out toward the trees to try to see if they could identify the source of the flying branch.

At the same time they each saw a large, hairy hand start to slowly come around the trunk of one of the big trees on this side of the house. Crystal and Freddie looked at each other quickly in disbelief, then back out toward the hand that had passed in front of the tree and grabbed onto it somewhat.

"It's impossible," said Freddie.

The fingers of the huge hand slowly unclenched the tree and pointed straight out in the direction of Crystal and Freddie, holding still for several moments.

"There he is," said Crystal, simply. As she spoke she felt a rush of emotions, like something bottled up had been uncorked and was about to flow freely. Recognizing the significance of what they were seeing, Crystal felt some tears coming to her eyes.

"He actually came back," said Freddie in a hushed tone, "and as usual his timing is impeccable," he said, referring to his own petty, mouthy insults that he had tossed at his sister.

Seeing their friend again unexpectedly after all these years was nearly overwhelming.

"We're here," Crystal shouted with a somewhat warbling voice toward the creature. "And we're really glad to see you," she added a bit more resolutely.

The large fingers flattened out against the bark of the tree again, then slid back completely behind the tree. Within a few seconds the kids heard a familiar rustle of leaves as a huge dark shape moved away toward the deeper woods. They could see it increasing in speed as the volume of sound decreased, and just like that it was totally gone.

Crystal and Freddie stood still, staring at the spot where the creature was last visible.

After several silent minutes, Crystal was the first to speak. "Well, he sure is back, isn't he?"

Freddie was still deeply affected by what they had just seen.

"I...I can't believe it," he said. "I never thought we'd see him again."

The brother and sister continued to stand still for some time.

Crystal eventually suggested, "Uh, maybe we should think about getting back to the party."

Freddie was still frozen in place.

"Yeah, I guess so," he said. "But you know what? Maybe it's *my* turn to write a song about him."

It was suddenly looking like this might turn out to be the best summer the kids had spent together in years.

ABOUT THE AUTHOR

DON SHEARER has had a lifelong interest in Sasquatch. He follows cryptid hominid research and current reported sightings throughout the U.S. In addition to being a writer and editor for health and wellness organizations, he is also an award-winning comedy music composer. In fact he has written a number of songs specifically about the Big Guy including *Bigfoot Ate My Book Report*, *Insufferable Shag-Bag* and *Sasquatch In My Pumpkin Patch*. Don lives in the desert Southwest where many mysterious occurrences have taken place amidst the wide open spaces and big sky. He and his wife Barbara roam the forests of northern New Mexico and surrounding areas to observe the wildlife of the region...including the ever-elusive and mysterious Sasquatch.

Don extends many thanks to Brian Cundle for the beautiful Sasquatch, kids and forest art.

85833260R00090

Made in the USA
Middletown, DE
27 August 2018